The Zambezi Chronicles:

The Contract

I0520230

Dwight Kopp

The Zambezi Chronicles: The Contract

Copyright © 2013 Dwight Kopp

ISBN 978-0-9895853-2-3

The Zambezi Chronicles: The Contract

eBook Copyright © 2012, Print Copyright © 2013 Dwight Kopp

The Zambezi Chronicles: Critical Fault

eBook Copyright © 2012, Print Copyright © 2013 Dwight Kopp

The Zambezi Chronicles: Cover of Darkness

eBook Copyright © 2012, Print Copyright © 2013 Dwight Kopp

Cover design by Doe and Dwight Kopp

All rights reserved. No part of this book may be reproduced or transmitted in any form or by any means, electronic or mechanical, including photocopying, recording, or any information storage and retrieval system, without prior written permission of the author.

#

All characters in this novel are fictitious. Any resemblance to actual persons, living or dead, is purely coincidental. While the geographic context of this story is true, all characters and situations are products of the author's imagination.

www.facebook.com/dwightkoppbooks

For Doe

Southern African Region

Zambezi River Region

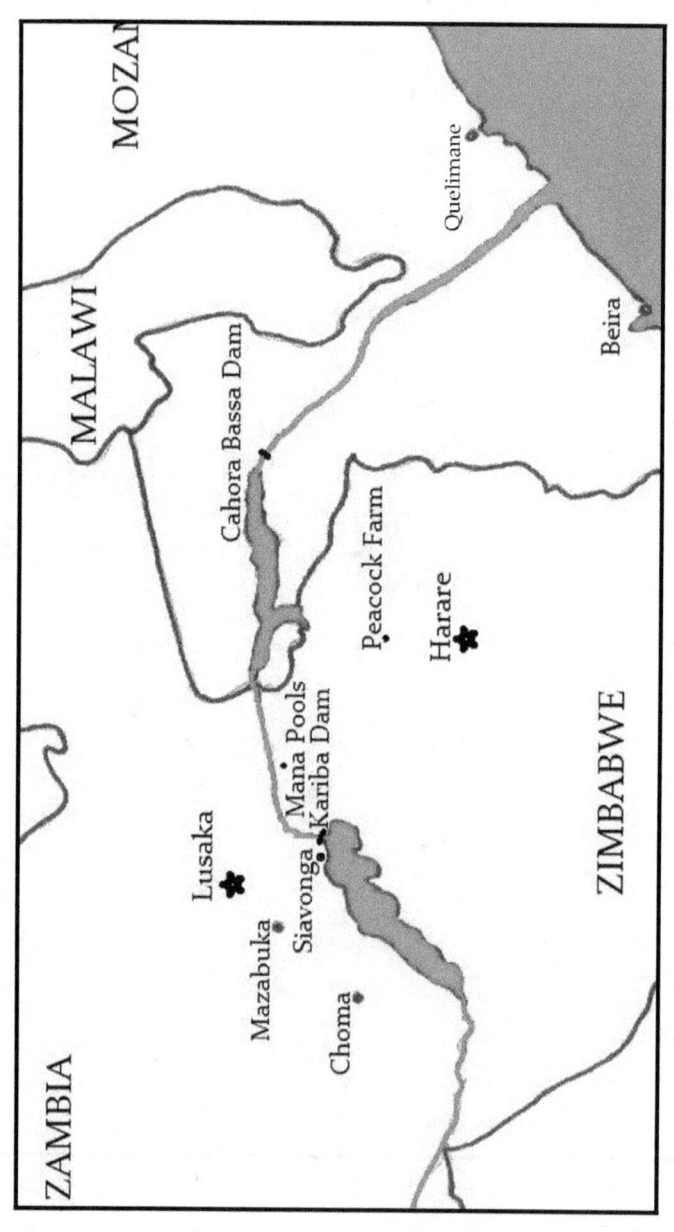

Chapter 1
2007
Southern Italy

Arturo Esposito paused before the door to smooth down his hair. The secretaries had already gone home, and the firm of Pinzini & Blaise was quiet. Only the company president remained in his office. It was better this way, Esposito thought; there would be no record of this meeting.

Esposito tapped lightly on the door and heard a soft, "Come."

He entered the office and pushed the door closed behind him. Pino Pinzini sat alone at his desk, bent over a file spread across polished mahogany. A lamp with a green shade squatted on the corner of his desk like a luminescent frog. Esposito waited.

"Sit there."

He settled into the leather chair opposite the desk and tried to make himself look comfortable. Esposito had planned this moment for years. Civil engineering paid reasonably well, but this was different. This was a coup d'état. Still the boss ignored him, engrossed in his own pile of paper.

Pinzini filled his chair, and his face, crisscrossed with the red lines of a heavy drinker, hung full and fleshy. Esposito waited for the man to put down his gold fountain pen and lift his head.

"We are alone. What do you want?" The boss finally spoke.

Esposito wet his lips. "I have a proposal for a construction contract," he paused, "and I already have a signature." Now he was sure to have his boss' attention.

"You and I both know that the ill-fated Malpasset Dam which burst in 1959 may not have been engineered correctly. It is openly speculated that minor, localized earthquakes precipitated by the nearby blasting was enough to cause the fatal crack. Still, the dam's failure was ruled an act of God."

"Go on," the boss ordered.

"The same year Malpasset failed, another much larger hydroelectric project between Zambia and Zimbabwe had just been completed. The Kariba Dam on the Zambezi River. What is not commonly known is that the engineer for both of these projects was the same Frenchman, one Cesar Fournier. Kariba remained, for a long time, the largest man-made reservoir in the world. 186 billion cubic meters of water."

Esposito reached into his attaché case and removed a brown envelope. Carefully, he pulled out a legal document printed on official Pinzini & Blaise letterhead, dated three months into the future. "This affidavit carries the official seal of the Republic of Zimbabwe and the signature of the Honorable Cedric Banda Mwanyisa. He holds the title of president but functions like a dictator."

The leather chair squeaked as Pinzini leaned forward.

"This document calls for the construction of a new dam across the Kariba Gorge. It awards the project to Pinzini & Blaise." Esposito placed the sheaf of paper under the frog lamp.

"How much?" Pinzini asked.

"Four billion US dollars."

The man's fat fingers gently came to rest on the contract. "But there is already a dam there."

Esposito smiled. "A small matter. It will not last long."

The boss leaned back in his chair and pulled a fat cigar from his coat pocket, drawing it habitually under his nose. He carefully snipped the edges and held a lighter to the end. Blue smoke mingled with the green lamp light and seemed to hang suspended in time as Pinzini thought.

The boss stared at the young man before him. "And how do you propose we make way for this new dam?"

Esposito continued. "Since the construction of Kariba Dam, reservoir-induced seismic activity has become a known phenomenon and is figured into tolerances for new construction. Several scientists have published reports on earthquakes resulting from the excessive pressure of a reservoir's water weight along fault lines. It will not be difficult to feed these findings to the press as a possible cause for the dam's failure. The scientists' words will sound prophetic, and the actual cause of failure will disappear in the academic haze of engineers who like to pretend that what they build will last forever."

"And what will be the *actual* cause of failure?" Pinzini asked.

"Several times in the last century, the Zambezi River Authority has had to open the spillway gates to release excess water from unseasonably high rainfalls in the Zambezi watershed. According to confidential reports I have accessed, Kariba is no longer cleared to use all six gates. The resulting vibration in the dam wall is unsafe. If someone were to make a few structural 'improvements,' those vibrations would be enough to cause a collapse."

3

Pinzini grunted and a smiled played on the corners of his mouth around the cigar. "Four billion US dollars," he muttered to himself.

"I should add," said Esposito, "the World Bank would front a loan insured by the United Nations and the Americans who will rise in support of the suffering people of Africa. The media will ensure the world gets a front-row seat to the disaster. The media love disasters."

"Will the World Bank front the money for a new construction project with all this talk of earthquakes?"

Esposito leaned back in his chair. "Aaah, but improved anti-quake technology has been developed that protects a dam from all but the most powerful quakes." He paused. "Besides, key signatures can be bought, and if the World Bank will not, the Asian Development Bank will jump at the investment opportunity.

"The press will write its own story. For now, I need your signature to close the deal."

The boss drew on his cigar and looked skeptically at the engineer, "What else will you need?"

"I sourced the necessary demolition materials but will need an anonymous source to purchase them, so they can't be traced. The operation itself requires two people. Aside from an underwater pneumatic drill, all the rest can be rented in Zambia."

"Who knows of this?"

"Aside from Mwanyisa, we are alone."

Esposito reached forward for the document, but the boss put his plump hand down on it, smiled; another line appeared over his eyes. "What does the old monster want?"

4

Esposito was ready for this. "Not much. Only three percent of the project cost, but he will also skim international aid that floods his country afterward. By planning ahead he will appear a capable leader when disaster strikes. In doing so, he hopes to be embraced by the international community, enticing outside investors once again. If he manages the aid well, Mwanyisa will also win back the admiration of his people and secure his long-term rule. Or so he thinks."

Chapter 2
Peacock Farm, Zimbabwe

Stuart Hall slammed the front door and threw the paper down on the entry-way desk. He pulled his hat off and ran fingers through his hair.

"What is it?" Kathy stood in the parlor doorway. She was almost 50 but hid her years well. The African sun agreed with her white skin and seemed to add color without wrinkles.

"We've received an offer for sale." He spoke the words like they were bitter pills.

Kathy leaned against the doorway. "So, it has finally come."

"Land repatriation." He picked up the paper and read. "The *fine* government of Zimbabwe extends the offer of four million Zimbabwean dollars for the purchase of your land and home. The offer has been extended because of the *generosity* of the Zimbabwean government and her people." He laughed without humor. "Four million," he repeated. "With current exchange rates, our farm is worth less than a loaf of bread."

"What are we going to do?" Kathy moved over to look at the signature.

"Nothing. I'm not going to let that vulture take away our farm. We've invested too much to walk away."

"Are we safe?" She folded her arms to hide her shaking hands. "You know what they did to the Clements and the Farleys. And the –"

"The Shona here are loyal to us. We've been good to them. I'll make sure I talk to the headmen first thing tomorrow. It'll be fine. He's already told me they don't want us to leave. I am their shade tree."

"You are right. We'll be fine. Everyone else has been driven away, harassed until they gave in; homes burned to the ground. But we, alone in all Zimbabwe, will be fine." Her voice shook ; she stopped.

Stuart moved to her, and put his arm around her shoulder. For years they had watched as Mwanyisa systematically removed white farmers throughout the country and gave the land to whomever he wanted. They watched the agrarian based economy grind to a halt. They hoped the foolishness would stop before it reached them. It had been a foolish hope.

They moved to the verandah and looked over their farm. The sun rested low in the sky, above the wood lot at the far corner. In the distance they could hear lowing cattle and the sharp whistles of herd boys. Around the house the fragrance of pink and white frangipani mingled with the smell of earth, freshly washed by rain.

Kathy wiped her eyes and rang a bell. The maid appeared.

"Suzie, do bring us two Malawi shandies. No bitters for me."

Suzie nodded quickly and disappeared into the house.

"We'll ride this out. Old Mwanyisa can't last forever." Stuart bent over to untie his boots.

"I'm so glad the children are living in Harare. Though I don't know how much longer anyone can last. I'm just glad we have some money saved at Barclays." She looked past the screen to the broad valley before them. "Sometimes I don't know what I want. I want to stay. And yet, I can't see staying in this place where a tyrant defines every corner of our lives. Sheila called from Harare saying they can't find milk anymore. All kinds of deliveries are shutting down because of the fuel shortage."

Suzie carried in the drinks. A slice of lime perched on the corner of each glass.

"Ndatenda," Stuart thanked her. "How is your father these days?" he asked the maid.

Suzie stopped and stared at the ground. "He is not well. The malaria has come back."

"Oh Suzie, you should have told me." Kathy got up from her seat. "Come with me. I'll get you some muti from the cabinet." Kathy turned to her husband. "I'm sending Suzie home early tonight."

"Good idea." Stuart took a long drink from his glass and tried to relax.

He heard the telephone ring in the hall but ignored it. Kathy would get it.

Chapter 3
Harare, Zimbabwe

Sheila Smith closed the gate and shook rain off her umbrella before opening the door. The rain started after she left the little produce market a few blocks away. The dogs didn't bark. They never did like the rain. Still there was something comforting about their ferocious barking when she came home.

"Hello, Daniel?" she called. The house was quiet. He was probably out trying to work another deal with the minister of tourism. Everything was getting more complicated these days. He wanted to launch his new business by now, but the government red tape was endless. Zimbabwe certainly needed tourists and the influx of foreign exchange. But most government officials were afraid to do anything for fear of incurring the disfavor of Mwanyisa. Especially as it related to a business owned by a white man. Even if that white man happened to be a Zimbabwean citizen.

Sheila dropped her shopping bag on the kitchen table and put the kettle on for tea. It would be nice to have a quick shower and change before he got home. She decided to put the groceries away later.

She took off her shoes and padded across cool tiles toward the master bedroom. A puddle pooled under a window in the living room. Must have blown open during the storm. The rains had finally come. She pushed the window shut and opened doors to the veranda. A cool breeze blew through the house.

Maybe the Rhodesian Ridgebacks had escaped to the garden shed before the rain, she thought. More likely, Daniel had taken them out for a walk, and they would all be back shortly, dripping wet, and marking up the clean tile. Martha, the maid, was off today, and Sheila didn't want to clean up after wet dogs.

She walked back to the kitchen to fetch her tea. Nothing like a cup of tea on a rainy day. She sugared it and carried it to the bathroom.

They moved to the house—a wedding present from her parents—after their honeymoon. It was perfect for two. They were glad to be settled in, though she wished she could have more of Daniel. After the wedding they vacationed in the north at Mukambi Lodge along the Kafue River in Zambia. The game viewing was fantastic, though they had spent much of their days in their rondoval exploring each other. Then they would slip into the pool or move to the wet bar, share a drink and watch the hippos call from the water.

Just last evening they poured over the pictures again on his laptop. The images of the Kafue National Park were astounding. "Daniel, do you think we should move to Zambia instead?" she asked, not for the first time. He had been working tirelessly to find a niche in the tourist business, but the machinery of Zimbabwe ground away at their options. Fuel shortages, rising crime and political red tape made start-up tourism difficult. Daniel's determination scared her. She would have loved an easier way forward, but somehow, his single-mindedness kept him from considering other options. Thankfully, they had enough money from savings and wedding gifts to keep them going for a year or so.

It would all be okay.

Zimbabwe was home, after all. She stared at herself in front of the bathroom mirror. Like her mom, Sheila was petite. Hair almost brown. Serious green eyes. She set her tea on the vanity and undid the buttons on her dress, let it fall around her ankles and stepped into the shower. She stepped under the water, felt it run down her body, washing off the day.

She heard a door open. "Hi. I'm in the shower, luv." She talked loud enough for Daniel to hear. "I've just been down to that little market. Prices were terrible, but I found some tea." She doused the water, reached out for a towel and pulled back the shower curtain.

A huge black man stood watching from the bathroom doorway. Shiela let out a short, frightened scream.

He held her flowered tea cup, sipping it while he waited. A pair of ugly green grenades dangled from his belt like hideously misshapen testicles.

The man's face was profoundly black, more reflective of the tribes of central Congo than Zimbabwe. It held a meanness and clarity that left no questions. A fleshy, pink, sickle-moon scar hung unmoving in the black sky of his forehead.

"What do you want?" she demanded, trying to keep her voice from shaking. "Where is Daniel?"

"That is no concern of yours." He folded his arms. Muscles moved across his chest under camouflage green. "Get dressed." She had to squeeze past him, touch him, smell him, to get to her clothes. Trying to keep herself covered, she pulled on shorts and a shirt.

"Where is my husband?" She felt more confident, now, though the man appeared to have no interest in her body.

He finished her tea, and set the cup gingerly on the dressing table. "As I said, that is not your concern." He opened her wardrobe, and pawed through her underwear, dropping them one by one on the floor by his polished combat boots, looking for something.

He found her handgun, pulled it out and opened the magazine. Shiny brass bullets blinked from their places.

"What do you want?" Sheila felt the trembling begin in her chest. "Tell me what you want? My husband will be home soon." She glanced toward the door, willing Daniel to appear.

"Daniel has been detained." The man lifted the gun and sighted her in. The trembling grew worse. She sat down on the bed, but stood again, not wanting to give him any ideas. He noticed and chuckled. Her fear seemed to bring him pleasure. "This is a nice weapon, madam." He lowered the gun. "Why would you need to keep this with your panties? Are you afraid of your husband?"

She struggled to think. "I don't know. My father gave it to me. Said I should keep it." Her words came in a rush.

"Ah, yes, your father. Mr. Stuart Hall." He condescended to speak the name, then walked toward the window and looked out. "You have a nice house, here, madam."

"Thank you," she replied stupidly.

He looked disapprovingly at her. "You must remember to keep the windows closed, so you don't let in the rain."

The thought that the man had been in her house ever since she returned increased her panic. She shot a glance outside. "Where is Daniel?" she asked again, trying to sound firm.

The man moved. Stood directly in front of her. She could smell him again. Feel his hot breath. He drew back a hand and smashed it against the side of her face. Sheila's eyes exploded with white

12

specks of light. She reeled, fell back on the bed, and tumbled onto the floor.

"Daniel is awaiting trial." The man raised his voice only slightly.

"Trial? What are you talking about?" Tears smeared across her stinging face. She stood, tasting blood on her lip.

He looked her over distastefully, slipped the magazine from her gun and dropped it next to the scattered lingerie. Didn't answer.

"So why are you here?" she asked. Rage fought with panic. "What have you done with Daniel?"

"I am here because your father has been given an offer." He reached out and wiped at the blood on her lip. Then he put the finger in his mouth and sucked it off. "He needs to make a wise choice."

"What do you mean?" she asked. "What does that have to do with Daniel?" She tucked her hands under her armpits. Tried to stop the shaking.

"Madam, it has everything to do with Daniel." The man reached into his pocket, dropped two spent shells on the dressing table and left. The brass casings set her mind spinning.

The front door closed and Sheila remembered the dogs.

Chapter 4
Peacock Farm, Zimbabwe

The phone kept ringing. "Kathy? Can you get that?" Stuart got up from the wicker chair and strode across the zebra skin to the phone.

"Hello?" Static filled his ear. He shoved the receiver back into its cradle. "Damn phone lines." Immediately, the phone rang again.

"Hello?" Stuart listened, paled and slumped into a nearby seat. He pushed the phone away from his face and shouted. "Kathy! Come quick, something has happened."

He listened into the receiver, knowing that the sobbing on the other end of the line was Sheila. For a long time, she didn't speak.

"Daddy, they have Daniel," she managed.

"What?" Stuart's knuckles whitened. "Who?"

"I don't know who he is, but he killed the dogs." The voice was choked. Frances, her brother, had given them the dogs. A wedding gift.

"Are you hurt?" Stuart asked.

"They took Daniel." She fought on, trying to hold back hysteria. "He said something about an offer. Said you needed to make a 'wise choice.' What is he talking about?"

Stuart fell silent. Kathy stood in front of him.

"What is happening?" she demanded.

"We are being blackmailed." He covered the mouthpiece. "They are holding Daniel."

"Hold on, luv," he said. " I know what they want. I'll come get you right away. Then we can talk, okay? Pack for a few days, and stay inside until I come."

"Daddy, I'm frightened." Her voice seemed tiny on the phone. He still struggled to see her all grown up and married. It didn't seem that long ago when she followed him around the farm, holding onto the hem of his shorts.

"I'll be there as soon as I can."

Chapter 5
Southern Italy

The boxy limousine breezed along beside the sparkling Mediterranean. Arturo Esposito should have been enjoying the ride, but the prospect of meeting the mafia sat on his stomach like his mother's three cheese tortellini. Pinzini, his boss, had made all the arrangements and insisted he go. Who was he to refuse?

Esposito stared at rows of pencil thin trees running off at angles from the motorway, marking the ancient boundaries of various estates. He adjusted his bow tie and tried to relax. It wasn't every day that someone had an appointment with a mafia boss. The man was Ciro Michi, one of Pino Pinzini's 'brothers.' Esposito wasn't sure of their exact relationship. Perhaps they attended school together. Maybe the military. It didn't much matter. What did matter was that Pinzini trusted the man. Ciro Michi would provide the field operatives Esposito needed as well as the demolition powders he requested.

Ciro Michi came to power as an importer of girls who served without pay in his many high-class brothels in Italy. Michi further solidified his empire by keeping careful photographic records of those who sampled his wares, to be available should he need a 'favor.' Some said Ciro Michi was owed a million favors. His clients came from the largest and strongest families in Italy and served in the country's highest political offices.

Occasionally, someone would try to shake off Michi's influence, but it never ended well.

The limousine turned, left the highway and passed through vineyards that folded into the horizon. According to Pinzini, Ciro Michi farmed for a living, but the fruit of his other ventures made his fortune. The limousine stopped at an iron-gate. The driver presented credentials to a grunt whose weapon flashed conspicuously under a silk tweed.

Chapter 6
Harare, Zimbabwe

Sheila found the dogs.

Rufus lay by the shed. A purple bougainvillea, heavy from rain, drooped over him. Blood pooled beneath his head where a single bullet had pierced his skull. Sheila sat in the grass and pulled the dead dog onto her lap.

"My poor baby." She rocked the hound and stroked the funny ridge of hair on his back. Its legs already growing stiff.

"Molly?" she called softly—not wanting to know. Didn't want to see another. "Come Molly."

A copper tail sticking out from behind the garden shed twitched gently. Sheila slid Rufus off her lap and crawled across the grass to his mate. A bleeding red eye glared out from the dog's midsection. Molly wagged her tail weakly.

Sheila had seen death before. Already the dog's eyes had begun to gloss. Sheila lay next to Molly, talking softly to her and stroked her head until the wagging stopped. Molly stretched against the pain in her gut and whined softly. Then the light in the dog's eyes went away.

Sheila heard a honk at the gate and the shout of her father's voice.

She stood, numb, and hurried through the house to the veranda. Her father unlocked the gate with his own key and pulled his red-dust covered Peugeot up the short drive.

Sheila stayed on the screened porch and waited for him to come inside. Her mind stopped putting things in order. She wanted someone else to do it for her.

Stuart charged up the stairs and pushed aside the screen door. "What happened?" He froze and stared with horror at the blood on her shorts and hands. The next moment he was pulling her into his arms.

"Why are you bleeding?" He tried to keep the panic and rage out of his voice.

"They've killed the dogs, Daddy," Sheila said simply. She looked at her lap. "It's their blood, not mine."

The same strong arms that carried calves on the farm now lifted her. She leaned against his wide shoulders and could see the sun spots on this worried face. "You're going to come home with us for a while, my dear. I'll contact someone here to find Daniel. It will all be okay, luv."

He settled her in the passenger seat, went back to the house for her bag and locked the door as he left. He maneuvered his large frame into the car.

"We're with you now, my dear." His soft words warmed the scared place inside her. "We'll get you home and cleaned up."

"What do they want?" Sheila's tears fell unfettered. "What did Daniel do?"

His knuckles whitened on the wheel. He stared at the road, concentrating on potholes. "Nothing. I'm going to see my attorney tomorrow. He is good. He'll be able to help."

Chapter 7
Peacock Farm, Zimbabwe

Stuart's shotgun stood loaded beside the bed, but he wasn't sleeping. When he closed his eyes, Sheila appeared, covered in blood, cowering on the veranda in Harare. Every time the dogs barked outside he checked the windows, staring off into the darkness, trying to tell the shadows apart from the specters of his own imagination.

He had lived in Zimbabwe all his life. Born and raised under a jacaranda tree, he used to say. His grandfather had been the first to move to Zimbabwe from England, but that had been a different time.

Stuart knew enough about the politics of Africa to have few illusions. Still, Africa's irresistible attraction kept him longer than most other white farmers. Some had left early, sensing the tide turning against them. His own brother made a fresh start in New Zealand. At the time, he felt betrayed as if his brother was giving up on his country, giving up hope. Now he wasn't so sure.

The dogs settled themselves outside. Nothing was out there. No one was watching. At any rate, he couldn't see anything. Some consolation.

He padded to the kitchen for a drink. Water droplets sweating off the glass dripped onto his bare toes.

It would soon rain. He could see the lightning flash on the horizon, momentarily illuminating giant silver-gray clouds thrust up against the backdrop of stars. "Africa," he whispered, "why do you have to be so damn beautiful?"

He retrieved his shotgun, returned to the veranda and settled into a chair. The cold gun leaning against his leg.

The distant clouds grew closer, shutting out the starlight and deepening the darkness. Sweat rolled down Stuart's chest as he dozed. The night air stilled—breathless and waiting.

Clouds birthed lightning. The sky exploded. Night flashed to day. Great sheets of rain turned the ground into slippery mud and rivulets of brown water that wormed their way into Stuart's sleep. The rivulets coalesced into freshets and streams until the rushing water covered Peacock Farm, surged around the standing trees and carried away the soil. Water swirled black, menacing the foundation of the house. Fastened to the ground, Stuart watched in horror as the land disappeared around him. Somewhere in the distance he could hear Sheila screaming, but he couldn't move.

Another flash erupted. The ground shook. The air buzzed and hot thunder echoed against the iron gates of hell.

Stuart's glass slipped from his hand and shattered at his feet. He woke with a start, heart racing, sweat-soaked hand reaching for the gun. The rising sun pierced grey clouds. Stuart listened for the sound of Sheila's voice and heard only the growl of far-away thunder. It had been a dream.

He bent over, picked the glass bits off the floor and set them out of the way.

"Good morning bwana." Suzie entered the veranda, dressed as usual in a blouse and a mismatched brightly colored, cotton cloth wrapped about her. Suzie offered him tea.

"Ndatenda, Suzie," He took the tea, anxious for something to wash away the bad taste. "How is your father?"

Suzie stared fixedly at the ground. "He is late," she replied.

Stuart's teacup stopped half way. "Oh Suzie. I am sorry," he said.

Suzie nodded faintly.

"I want to help with funeral expenses. I'll send the boys around this morning with an extra bag of maize for the mourners. You should go home now and take care of your mother. You didn't need to come today my dear." He rose and shook her hand tenderly expressing his condolences. "He was a good man."

"Thank you, bwana." She turned and left quietly.

Stuart leaned against the veranda's knee-wall. What next? He should stop by to see Suzie's mother, but first he had to figure out what to do about his son-in-law.

The young man had practically grown up with the Hall family. Stuart hardly remembered seeing Francis, his own son, without Daniel. Daniel's mother ran the neighboring farm while his father led safaris for the rich and famous during hunting season. It was a hard kind of life, but they managed, somehow. The two lads roamed with the herders, speaking Shona like black boys and shooting at anything that moved with their homemade slingshots. When they got older, the two sometimes joined Daniel's father on safari whenever they could convince their mothers that it would be enough of an educational experience to justify skipping school.

Somewhere in there, Sheila burst into womanhood. Then out of the blue, this young Daniel was asking if they could marry. It had been quite a shock. As her father, he allowed some reservations against the man who married his only daughter, but those now seemed insignificant. The man in jail was his daughter's husband.

He would have to do something, but he wasn't ready to lose the farm.

Chapter 8
Harare Prison, Zimbabwe

The shining mass of razor-barbed wire trolled twin rows of rusting chain-link fence. Tin from the sliding board had long since been scrabbled. The derelict remains of the slide's skeleton, naked and rusting, rotted on the prison parade ground.

The wards formed a complete square enclosing an inner courtyard swept clean and bare and boasting only a single remaining tree. Once children had skipped rope here and played Mancala with seeds from the pepper corn trees. Three hundred blue and white uniforms with grey socks and black shoes. Boys talked about the girls, and the girls plaited hair and pretended not to notice. There had been more trees then. These had since been chopped down to feed the warden's cooking fire.

Crude towers of wood and corrugated iron guarded two corners of the outside fence. Soldiers stationed in each tower surveyed the parade ground, hands casually resting on weapons. A second pair of guards patrolled the perimeter, chatting amiably and ignoring emaciated prisoners soaking up their allotted hour of sunshine. Another boring day.

At midmorning, a white government Mercedes pulled up to the gatehouse. The soldier snapped to attention and let them through to the interior office building. A man without a uniform unfolded himself from the passenger seat. A government man. The buttons of his white shirt struggled to hang on across his middle. He leaned against the car and laughed at the staring prisoners staring. He pulled a pack of cigarettes from his pocket and held one between his lips. A gold ring on his little finger flashed the sunlight.

"Good morning, sir." The warden stepped from a square building and approached the vehicle.

"Yes, it is. Portuguese cigarette?"

"Thank you." The warden lit his smoke on the visitor's match.

"We have a guest for your facility. A white man." He nodded toward the car.

"Who is it?"

"A political prisoner."

The warden bent over and glanced inside. A maize bag hooded the man's face, tied about his neck with a stained piece of sisal twine.

The government man lowered his voice, "He is not to be harmed. He will be here only a few days, but he is not to know this."

The warden nodded. "I will find him a place."

Chapter 9
Southern Italy

The driver parked on the cobblestone around the fountain pond. In the center, a stone woman held an amphora above her shoulders. Water spilled from the vase, ran down her naked body and splashed on lilies crowding around her knees. Arturo Esposito stepped from the limousine. Rows of flowering citrus trees fanned out from manicured gardens surrounding the mansion. Blooming wisteria cascaded from pergolas lining the path.

A security guard stepped from the shade, ran his hands brusquely under Esposito's coat and down his legs. Satisfied, he pulled out a cellphone and punched a few numbers.

A bead of sweat ran down Esposito's chest toward his stomach. He tried to ignore it. Today he was on his way to being a made-man.

He was led through a garden beside the house. Irises played along a pool's edge and creeping ivies lined ancient flagstone. They turned a corner where the guard paused. In a gazebo, nestled near a waterfall concealed by greenery, a silver-haired man sat alone, reading.

Ciro Michi ignored their approach. He wore a white cotton shirt with a tailored jacket. A hat of the same color rested on the seat beside him. Michi was smaller than Esposito anticipated. His guide coughed quietly and retreated. The fragrance of wisteria blossoms lingered. Esposito waited.

"I hear you are a businessman," Michi said without looking up from his book.

"Yes," Esposito replied.

"I, too, am a man of business." Michi closed his book, looked over. "You have been working with my old friend Mwanyisa."

Esposito nodded.

"Please, forgive me. Sit down." Michi waved him into the gazebo. "I received your message."

Michi held up the ancient volume. "Shakespeare. The sonnets are my favorite. Do you read much, Mr. Esposito?"

Esposito swallowed and shook his head. "I'm afraid I'm not much of a reader. I've always been better with numbers."

"Yes. You are good with numbers."

A happy squeal followed a child dancing down the path. The embroidered roses on her dress and fine black curls flounced along with her song. She stopped when she saw them. Fingers went into her mouth and her eyes grew round.

"Come here my little olive." Michi held out his hand to the girl, who came shyly, chewing on her fingers. She climbed the two steps into the gazebo, stood before the old man and ignored Esposito.

"Why are you running down the path?" Michi asked.

"Playing," she said through wet fingers.

"And what were you playing?" Michi asked, taking the child by the arm and drawing her onto his lap.

"Fairies." She looked into his eyes. "A pretty blue one." She pointed down the path.

"I see," Michi nodded seriously. "Did you know a fairy has been hiding in my pocket?"

"A fairy?" she whispered, not wanting to scare it off.

"Yes." He opened his jacket and let her peek inside. A polished wooden pistol grip protruded from a concealed holster. "Have you ever touched a fairy before?" The girl shook her head and curls danced beneath ribbons. "Then, perhaps, you had better let me check first, just so we don't surprise her." Michi hooked one finger over his inside pocket and pulled it open, peering cautiously over the side. The girl's finger left her mouth and she leaned gingerly forward, expecting the fairy to come darting out.

Michi's face grew serious. "Oh dear," he said. "I'm afraid she might have gone away." He looked sadly at the child. Her lip quivered.

Michi turned back to the pocket and reached his hand inside and fished around. "Wait! She left you something." He withdrew his hand and held the closed fist up for her to see, then opened his fingers to reveal a beautiful tear-shaped candy, the color of honey.

The girl gasped and reached out for the treat.

"Now. Run along my little olive. See if you can catch her and give her a kiss."

At the steps she stopped and turned back to Michi. She walked over to him, stood on her tiptoes and kissed him on the cheek. Then with a bounce of curl and tulle and lace, she was gone.

Ciro Michi watched her go.

Esposito sat without speaking.

"My daughter." His smile faded and he turned back to Esposito. "Family is everything." He picked up his Shakespeare and opened to the page marked by a single rose petal. "I will get you what you need."

The meeting was over.

Chapter 10
Harare Prison, Zimbabwe

Daniel Smith woke to the grind and rasp of a door opened and closed again. The rank odor of fecal matter and piss wormed its way into his clothing. No window. No pail for waste. He moved, bones aching from the concrete floor, and cursed himself. He should have listened to Sheila and relocated to South Africa or north to Zambia. The not knowing; the wondering about her. It was too much.

Down the hall, another prisoner coughed. A grinding tuberculous sound, like the door, followed by a hock and spit.

Daniel leaned into the corner opposite his own pile of shit. Fatigue fought with fear for his wife while unyielding iron bars pressed into his back. He rubbed hands over his scrubby face, trying to wake up enough to think through his options.

This didn't take long. After his arrest, no communication had been possible. The soldiers took his wallet and passport. No discussion. Nothing. Just the boring business of processing another prisoner. No personal effects allowed. Official rubber stamps. No eye contact. Shame. Fear. The penetrating buzz of a single fly beating itself to death on the ceiling. The slow, crowded air of the police station. Stacks of legal ledgers. Pink carbon copies in triplicate jammed on an iron spike. No records for the prisoner. Vague references to some illegal activity.

Daniel stood to stretch out the ache in his back. His cell faced a hall with no windows. Far away a rooster crowed. Soon hot sun would beat down on the tin roof and the smell of shit and sweat would swelter and make him nauseas again. He grabbed hold of the bars, pushed his face hard against them, tried to see. Tiny ants burrowed their way up through cracks in the concrete, making tidy piles of sand around their hole.

"Friend." A voice called down the hall. "Tell me of my Zimbabwe."

"Who are you?" Daniel replied.

"What does it matter? I am, like you, a prisoner." The man cherished each word. As if conversation was his only entertainment. His English was good. Probably educated in Harare before Zimbabwe began its long downward spiral.

"Why are you here?" Daniel asked again.

"Why is anyone here?" A musical laugh followed, unforced and comforting.

Daniel couldn't reciprocate. "Can you give me a name?" he said.

"A name? What do names matter? I am one of the forgotten."

"What do you mean?"

"Do you have a good memory, friend? Or have you also forgotten?"

"Look. I don't have time for riddles," Daniel shot back.

"You don't have time?" The gentle laugh again. "Time is all we have." A pause, and Daniel heard a shuffle as the man settled himself, a long contented sigh of a man used to prison.

Daniel pressed his forehead against the cool bars. "Look, I'm sorry. I don't know what I have or don't have. I don't even know

31

why I'm here. I don't know what is happening to my wife. She probably doesn't know where I am."

The man hissed his disapproval, a show of empathy. Daniel tried to picture him. In his mind, lines and frosted peppercorn hair framed the black face.

"Where are you from?" Daniel asked again. "You sound like a professor."

"I am from Harare. I am not a teacher. Perhaps that would have been better for me. And you? You are a white man, yes? For now, you are the only one here."

"Here? I don't even know where here is." Daniel wanted to lash out, kick the walls. Shout and scream. But he knew Africa. The impatient man will be made to wait. The impatient white man loses all respect. So he would wait. He would learn the game. He would play the few cards he had.

"This is a school." The voice spoke again. "At one time, students studied in these rooms. Now, the only education offered here is tyranny. This is one of Mwanyisa's unofficial prisons. Here, we do not exist. Yet, we are not without hope. God has not forgotten us." A pause. "You can call me Gideon."

"You a pastor?" Daniel said. "That last bit sounded dangerously like a sermon."

Another sigh. "A pastor? This country needs more than a pastor. It needs a Jesus. Or maybe a patriot."

"What do you mean?" Daniel asked. Talk to the voice, he told himself. There was, after all, nothing else to do.

"After I finished secondary school, I applied for a scholarship to John's Hopkins School of Medicine in the United States. When I finished my studies, I attended a forum hosted by the United Nations for international students in New York City. Students— mostly graduate students—participated in discussion on various topics from HIV and AIDS to the development of primary health care systems in rural areas.

"I remember little, but during lunch one day I sat at a table with some men who were discussing the situation in North Korea. One of them said something I shall never forget. 'If there is one thing we can conclude,' he said, 'even dictators rule by permission of the people.'"

Daniel gave a humorless chuckle. "I don't think he ever met our current president."

"Don't you see?" Gideon said. "Fear is what keeps a dictator in power, but fear is a shadow at sunset. When the sun is low, even small things cast a long shade. Fear is used in the absence of real strength. Today the people of Zimbabwe cower at a shadow, but few have had the courage to ask what it is that casts this shadow."

"And you figured it out?" Daniel asked.

"I have."

"What did you find?" Daniel rested his arms on rusting bars.

"I am not afraid," Gideon replied.

"Is that why you're in here?"

"Yes. When a man has no fear, a dictator has no power, and the dictator is threatened."

"What about your family? Don't you worry about them?"

There was a long silence before Gideon replied. "Not anymore."

"I am terribly sorry." Daniel wished he hadn't asked.

"My wife was a good and brave woman. It was with her blessing I pursued a political career in hopes of bringing an end to this fear. She knew it would be expensive, and she was not afraid to die. If she were still alive, it would certainly be harder for me to press forward. Now, I cannot stop. Her voice and the voice of my children compel me."

Daniel could hear the ache in Gideon's voice, and they sat for a while without talking. Then Gideon asked, "Are you going to stay in Zimbabwe?"

Daniel let out a snort of impatience. "Yes, but a lot of good it has done me. I can't seem to dig my way through the red tape to start a business. Even if I did, the country is such a wreck that I wonder if it is worth the trouble. My wife thinks I should have given up a while ago. I don't know what kind of a life I can build for her here, not to mention any children that might come along. Maybe I should have left a long time ago."

"So why did you stay?"

Daniel paused. "I knew a man, once, who walked down to the bar every day after work. Some said he was just thirsty, but for whatever reason, he drank a lot. Every day. He came to like the bottle so much that he stopped going to work altogether. Eventually he even stopped going home."

"You are a white man, but you speak like a black man," Gideon said.

"What do you mean?" Daniel asked.

"You speak in stories."

"Ya, I guess so. But you understand, eh? Africa is like the bottle. I can't seem to shake the habit. It is probably going to ruin my marriage. And I've only been married a few months. Agh. Shit." Daniel gave the bars of his cage a little shake.

"You are a patriot," Gideon said. It was not a question.

"Why did you stay?" Daniel asked.

"You ask a man in jail, 'Why do you stay here?' " Gideon laughed again. Simple, unhurried laughter. It reached out to Daniel and the absurdity caught hold, and he, too, laughed. It felt good.

"Maybe that is why they have put me in this cage," Gideon said. "They are afraid I will leave." He grew serious and continued. "I am here because, like you, I believe in Zimbabwe. I, too, have wondered if this is a foolish passion, but I remember what it has been."

"I had the chance to move to New Zealand before things got really bad," Daniel said. "I visited there. A beautiful country. But it felt like flirting with another man's wife."

"And so you came back to watch Zimbabwe die?"

"You talk like there is no hope. The country wouldn't be in this condition if a certain snake wasn't choking the life out of it."

"You are right. It is not dead. Instead, we are just waiting."

"Waiting for what?" Daniel asked.

Gideon's voice was barely a whisper. "We are waiting for someone to cut the head off the snake."

Daniel replied quietly. "So you are looking for an assassin?"

"No," Gideon said. "We are waiting for a patriot."

Chapter 11
Downtown Harare, Zimbabwe

Stuart Hall climbed the narrow block stairs to the second floor. Davison Chuma worked alone. Unable to pay his paralegal, her computer leaned in a useless pile by the wall. In its place sat a polished Royal typewriter. Vintage 1940. The city's all-too-frequent power-outages called for more practical methods of communicating.

"Thank you for seeing me." Stuart shook hands with Chuma. "How is your family?"

"We are well, thank you," Chuma replied. "I'm glad you have come. I have news for you."

"Great. Did you find him?"

"Yes. Daniel is being held on the outskirts of town. A place known as a destination for political prisoners. Few prisoners stay there long; most get the message and find other pursuits. Others are more persistent. I had a conversation with a man who knows the head warden. He does not know how long Daniel is being kept. The charges are the usual: 'illegal activity' and so on."

"That is ridiculous," Stuart said.

"Of course it is. The charges are not important in Daniel's case. We must discover what they want."

Stuart settled himself in the plastic chair across the desk from Chuma. The room's only window opened to a market below. The odor of dried fish and chatter of bartering filtered up from the street.

"Is he being treated well?" Stuart asked.

"For now. Anything can change in those places," Chuma replied. "How is your family?"

"Sheila is having a rough time, as you can imagine. So is Kathy." He lowered his voice. "There is more than what I told you over the phone. It appears the honorable government of Zimbabwe wants to purchase my farm."

Chuma's brow furrowed. "Land repatriation."

Stuart continued. "Daniel is being held as assurance that I will accept. I suppose someone in the president's circle has taken a liking to our farm." Stuart stood and walked to the window. "I haven't told Sheila about this. I don't want to put her in that position. There has to be another option."

"The number of options we have is directly related to the quality of our legal system. And our legal system..." his voice trailed off and he tapped his pen on the blotter. "You have seen how a termite colony consumes a stick on the ground? First they cover the stick in mud, then they eat the stick."

"Right," Stuart nodded. "Leaving only mud in the shape of a stick." He returned to his chair and slumped down.

Chuma shook his head. "In truth, there is no legal system. Just the empty shell of one that used to be."

"Do we have any recourse, then?" Stuart asked.

"Not exactly. We will have to make do."

"Is there any way to fight this?"

"Fight? Be careful with this word, my friend," he paused. "No. I don't think so." Chuma stared at his desk for a while then pulled off his black-rimmed glasses and rubbed his nose. "Perhaps there is another way."

"I'm listening," said Stuart.

"For now the president does what he wants. However, the legal machinery of our country is still in place, and while the president may be able to take what he wants, it will take him longer to get the legal title in hand." Chuma replaced his glasses and stood. "This buys us a little time."

"So what would you suggest?" Hall asked.

"The only way I can think this might work is to play along. Give the government some kind of assurance that you will leave the farm. Get Daniel back and leave the country before any title transfer documentation can be completed. You will have to leave immediately and inconspicuously."

"So that's it. Just run away?" Stuart sounded defeated.

"Yes and no." Chuma lowered his voice. "Hopefully, it is only a matter of time until Mwanyisa is replaced. If you are lucky, you can return to your country and your farm within the next few years. Besides, if the man who gets the farm thinks you have abandoned Zimbabwe, then what does he care if he does not have the title? There may yet come a time when justice is honored again. If that happens, you can return to Zimbabwe with your title in hand. The courts will honor it."

"And where should I go? What would I do? I'm not like you. I don't have a legal education I could use in some other country. Farming is all I know. It is all I ever wanted to know."

"That is true. Many farmers have gone north to Zambia. However, Zambia has extensive duties on goods and machinery that you bring into the country. Duties that are somewhat prohibitive."

"You are right there. I know a few people who moved to Mazabuka and have taken up sugar cane farming. They had to start over."

"Have you been to Mazabuka?" Chuma asked.

"Not really. Just through it on our way north for hunting."

"It is a good place. There are many Tonga, cousins to my tribe, the Gwembe. Yes, you may have to start over, but Zambia is more politically stable than our country. It is a choice you will have to make."

"Okay. Let's say we follow your plan. How can I handle the border crossing if someone figures out that I'm leaving without 'signing over' the land?"

"There are other ways to get into Zambia. Perhaps I can help you there as well. Besides it is not the legal business that pays these days. It is the illegal business."

"I'll talk it over with Kathy." Stuart stood and shook Chuma's hand. "I'll stop by later today to let you know what we've decided."

Chapter 12
Lusaka, Zambia

Sean Wolfe stood outside the bank on Cairo Road. The road effectively cut Lusaka in half, its traffic swirling around an island of red flamboyant trees between the north and south bound lanes. Under their shade, vendors hawked daily newspapers and old men sat on goat-skinned stools to talk. Wolfe nodded a greeting to the bank's armed guard and hailed a cab. The blue and white Fiat pulled to a stop. Wolfe negotiated the fare and handed directions to his driver.

They turned on Kalombo Road at the north end roundabout. The driver avoided the rain-filled potholes, and eventually pulled into the compound for the customs and clearing agent. Wolfe paid and stepped out of the cab.

Like most businesses in Lusaka, the customs house placed a premium on security. Tall iron gates bolted to grey cinderblock walls protected the perimeter. Security bars covered windows. Wolfe presented his card to the receptionist.

"Good morning." She looked as his card. "You may wait over there." She left her desk and walked into the back room.

Wolfe rubbed his hand across the stubble. The trip had been grueling, but he would have time for a shower later. Ciro Michi wanted the goods cleared through customs as soon as possible. Wolfe stared up at the dusty ceiling fan, stirring the air above him.

"Good afternoon, Mr. Wolfe." A man approached. "I am Kenneth Kanguya. You can follow me this way."

Kanguya led Wolfe to a crowded office. A row of reference manuals lined the back of his desk. Legal documents stacked in neat piles covered a well-used blotter. Kanguya closed the door behind them.

Wolfe waited until Kanguya sat down. "I brought the money you requested in your last email."

Kanguya's eyes brightened, and he licked his lips. "Thank you. I will prepare the chit here. No problems, no delays. Then we can go and inspect the goods. Just one pallet, is it?"

Wolfe nodded and Kanguya busied himself sorting through clearance documents and the accompanying legal disclosure. His calculator chattered as a white paper tongue spooled out from the feed. He tore it off, copied the number down and presented Sean with the final bill.

"You are from England?" Kanguya asked.

Wolfe turned to look at him. "I don't pay you to ask questions, okay?"

Kanguya shrugged and looked away from the man's cold blue eyes. "You understand," he said, "normally it takes quite some time for items to be cleared."

Wolfe pulled a bundle of US dollars from his backpack and counted them out carefully. He paused before adding a few extra bills to the pile.

"That is to cover any other delays you might encounter," Wolfe said. "I have found it to be a good business practice."

Kanguya took the money. "I'm sure we will have no problem taking care of your special needs here."

"Thank you. I was told you would be able to help." Sean returned the balance of the bills to his pocket.

They exited the office through a rear door, stepping into bright sunshine. A bare-dirt storage yard separated the office building from a corrugated warehouse. Kanguya removed the padlock and pushed the complacent metal door back along the side of the building. He switched on the lights. The holding warehouse contained a variety of goods waiting for clearance and pick up, from container loads to single plastic-wrapped pallets. Kanguya eyed the various piles and bits of machinery before stopping in front of a single wooden crate.

Kanguya double-checked the routing number against his paperwork. "Here it is. It just arrived this morning. Your timing is good. Should we arrange delivery?"

"I don't require delivery," Sean said. "I'll be around on Friday. Keep an eye on it, okay?"

Chapter 13
Siavonga, Zambia
On the shores of Lake Kariba

Sean Wolfe rented a car and drove south to Siavonga. The easy four-hour drive gave him time to sort out the days ahead. Lusaka's sprawl fell away behind him and traffic thinned. He passed the Livingstone turn off and its rough market with local fabrics flapping gaily in the breeze and continued south.

He had a few days to finalize his plans before he traveled back to Lusaka to pick up the other operative arriving from Rome or wherever. He had been told his assistant would be capable of performing the required service. The scattered bush began to thicken. Wolfe turned west and drove toward the lake. Like frozen giants, grotesquely shaped baobab trees towered above surrounding shrub. Wolfe passed the eroded settlements where goats stood on their toes to nibble the leaves from thorny acacia. The terrain changed and the forest thickened among the hills. Here and there the waters of the Kariba Lake flashed blue between trees. Wolfe marveled at the beauty of the place with a lake so abruptly placed among the hills.

After reaching Siavonga, Wolfe turned onto a graded gravel road. Smiling children moved to let him pass, waving excitedly. Some mud brick houses sported an occasional blue tarpaulin assisting the corrugated roof. Here and there, traditional huts with thatched roofs perched on limited level spaces, interlaced with dun-colored footpaths.

Wolfe turned into his resort. The hotel overlooked a lake now robed in the orange splash of sunset.

The Eagle's Rest catered to tourists and weekend travelers down from Lusaka. At one time, it had to compete with more lavish resorts on the Zimbabwean side of the lake. Traffic traveled across the border over the Kariba Dam, just a few miles away. Kariba Heights, the town on the Zimbabwean side sported some of the best resort hotels in Central Africa and had been a Mecca for international tourists and wealthy Africans. Not long ago, Zimbabwe had vibrated with health and money. People flocked to Kariba Heights to browse and marvel at a place where elephants occasionally walked through town, much to the irritation of shop owners. The resorts hobbled along, but the customer base had been gutted. International tourists generally avoid countries with dictators, even democratically-elected ones.

Wolfe checked in and ordered several cold beers delivered to his room. He unloaded his kit from the vehicle and walked down flagstone steps past the pool to his chalet—one of several scattered along the lakefront. The rooms all had patios where one could soak in the view of the lake shore.

Fathergill Island floated on the water. Below, a narrow beach marked the curve of the bay. A local fisherman, standing in his dugout, paddled to the far bank of the cove.

Wolfe entered his room and arranged the table. He unrolled a map and sat down. A few fat moths played catch around the light above his head, diving and landing with a thud on his notes before taking off again.

A blue line on his chart described the perimeter of the Kariba reservoir. The dam itself, a double curvature arch, located on the northeast corner of the map blocked the Kariba Gorge. Beyond the dam, water flowed freely again for the next 150 miles or so, until it joined another reservoir behind the Cahora Bassa Dam. The

Cahora Bassa Lake, itself almost 200 miles in length, held a remarkable 26 cubic miles of water.

Wolfe reached for the empty ashtray and placed it on the edge of the map to keep it from curling. Then his finger followed the line of the Zambezi River down toward the sea.

"Beautiful," he said.

Wolfe punched a series of numbers into a calculator, wrote the results on a pad and referenced a data sheet. He pulled another folder and withdrew an enlarged rendering of the dam wall itself. Using a ruler and red pencil, he put several marks below the spillway gates. The marks ran horizontal to the top of the dam but still below the water level on the lake side.

Wolfe placed one final mark off to the side of the dam—the edge of the dam's abutment on the Zambian side of the gorge. This spot was right next to the border crossing perched along the hill above the generating facility.

The final mark also identified a prime pressure point bearing the dam's weight. Arch dams were constructed on the same principle as the Roman aqueducts. The arch leans into the water and is anchored to bedrock by right and left abutments. These and the foundation bear the bulk of the weight. A slip on either side will bring the entire wall down. 'Insurance,' the Italian had told him. 'Plan B.'

Sean had done his own reading. Traditional embankment dams held back water by sheer mass. The Aswan Dam, for example. The genius of the double curvature arch dam was its minimalism. That had been the primary appeal to early investors. Though the project had been presented as a development scheme; its main purpose had been to provide quick, cheap electricity for the copper mines in what would become Zambia. Power for the people was not high on the ticket in the 1950's.

The money came from investors who expected returns. The dam had been built to provide electricity. It hadn't been constructed to withstand earthquakes. The disaster at Malpasset, in France, had given Esposito the idea of creating a break on a similar dam. Wolfe wondered why no one bothered to worry about the similarities between Malpasset and Kariba. I guess if you build it in Africa, no one pays attention, he thought.

Wolfe flipped through more notes. The drilling rig would arrive tomorrow. He had hired the men under a fictional company name to drill a well at the border crossing. They were, in fact, creating a leverage point directly between the left abutment and the granite bedrock. When they were finished Wolfe would drop in one of the Dexpan expansion plugs according to Esposito's directions— applying pressure at the fulcrum.

The powder came from a remote Chinese province but was used worldwide for demolitions where traditional explosives would destabilize nearby structures, or where blasting noise and flying rock was impractical. Before this job, he attended a trade show demonstration in Copenhagen.

In traditional applications, the powder was mixed with water and injected into strategically-located holes bored in the doomed structure. In a matter of 24 hours, the powder expanded to several times its size, cracking stone, concrete or marble. Funny, he thought, anyone can find it online. Strange that no one has thought to use it like this before. One didn't even need a license. One hundred US dollars would buy a 40 lb bag of the dry mix.

47

A moth landed hard on the map—buzzing wings spinning in circles upside down. Wolfe reached forward and flicked the moth across the room.

He sat back and rubbed his eyes.

Mr. Esposito had made a good choice.

Wolfe stood and walked to the door of his room, beer in hand. The sun had gone, and he could see the lights of fishing boats heading out for their nightly catch of a sardine-like silver fish known locally as *kapenta*. In the far distance, lightning blinked.

Chapter 14
Harare Prison, Zimbabwe

Rain pounded on tin, sheets of water sluicing off the ends. The sound obliterated any other noise within the prison, and Daniel leaned into his favorite corner. A slight breeze pulled some of the acrid stench from the room, replacing it with the smell of rain. He closed his eyes and imagined himself standing under the downspout of their little house, feeling the cold water coursing over his body, washing off the filth. He remembered Sheila stepping out of the cottage, dressed only in her swimsuit, smiling as she came to stand with him under the water, pressing herself against him. He opened his eyes and the image faded.

Daniel sighed. Something about Gideon's voice seemed hauntingly familiar, as if he were someone Daniel had previously met, but whose name he couldn't quite recall. Gideon. Gideon what?

Then in a rush he remembered. Television images. Interviews with a candidate. A sham election. Bribed international election officials. Oh God, Daniel thought, Gideon Chipinduka.

I'm in jail with the man who is supposed to be the president.

The doctor-candidate who dared to stand publicly against the tyranny of Mwanyisa. He felt a flush of shame at his own self-pity, and a rush of honor at being imprisoned next to a man brave enough to stand up to the dictator. Chipinduka had been chosen by the people but then disappeared after the 'election officials' declared a landslide victory in Mwanyisa's favor.

Everyone knew the truth.

Daniel felt a presence beside him.

"You must come with me." The warden spoke loud enough to be heard over the rain. He kicked the base of Daniel's cage and keyed the padlock.

"Collect your belongings." The guard turned and stood by the door of Daniel's cell. His automatic weapon slung over his shoulder.

Daniel looked around him. "What belongings?" he asked.

The warden made no reply.

"Where am I going?" Daniel did not move. Waited for an answer. He could feel fear grow again inside his stomach. He shifted his weight and stood up aching from the hard concrete floor. He took a moment to tuck in his shirt and fiddle with shoe laces. He had not removed the shoes for fear of them being stolen in his sleep. Daniel vaguely entertained fantasies of making a run for it, and he had wanted to be ready.

"Step this way." The guard motioned to the hall joining the cells.

Rain blew in through broken windows making puddles on cracked concrete. As they passed the next cell, Daniel looked down at his untied shoe and said, "Agh, sis man. I have to fix my laces." He bent down and locked eyes for a moment with the prisoner. Gideon had positioned his face close to the bars and Daniel saw him clearly in the low light.

"Mr. President," Daniel whispered. It was a declaration, not a question. Almost imperceptibly, Gideon nodded.

Daniel fussed with the knot and started chatting up the guard, completely ignoring the prisoner who sat just a few feet away. "I'm glad you came to get me out. I saw a file snake just outside my cell earlier this morning. If I see it again, I'm going to kill it. I don't like those things. Bad luck, eh? Maybe you can help me?" He chuckled and the guard grunted.

Daniel finished the knot and stood.

They entered a breezeway extending across an interior courtyard toward another parallel hallway. A blast of fresh air blew past them and Daniel felt has if he were actually breathing for the first time in days. Empty windows framed with rust and peeling orange paint stared at him from the courtyard. Ochre-colored dirt splashed up from the rains muddying the white-washed walls. The prison felt illegitimate and temporary. Save for the sound of rain and the passing growl of thunder, it seemed quiet. Daniel wondered if he and Gideon alone had been held in this place.

Mosquitoes swarmed Daniel's back as they entered another stale hall and crossed to a green door with a fading sign that read, "Head Master." The guard rapped twice.

"Kalibu," a voice answered.

The warden opened the door and waved him through. A visitor waiting for Daniel wore a faded, blue suit and leather shoes without socks. The shoes had once been red.

A fat man with black-rimmed glasses sat wedged on the far side of a desk. His gold beret rested beside him. A knotted, rope sash looped though epaulettes. Daniel noticed a missing button in the man's green jacket, but the hole was almost hidden by the white striped belt and square, medallioned buckle.

The uniform stood without acknowledging the prisoner, turned to a dented file cabinet and jerked on a drawer until it scraped open. Fingers walked deliberately through folders until he withdrew a form. He returned to his desk and began to fill in the release. He worked without comment, reached for a rubber stamp and pressed it hard into a tattered ink pad. The thump-thump of rubber stamps slammed onto the forms, the sound of officialdom. The uniform inspected the indicia under the window light.

The blue suit stood and received the proffered form. He turned to Daniel. "Mr. Smith, you must come with me."

Daniel followed him out. The blue suit turned to their guard escort and spoke a few words Daniel couldn't hear. He handed the guard a pack of cigarettes, and Daniel followed through the prison gates into freedom. The thunderstorm had passed and water dripped off trees lining the street outside. Daniel continued to follow, unsure of who the man was but the direction of travel was promising. To be outside again seemed completely surreal. His visitor avoided the puddles, but seemed more intent on getting out of sight and avoiding guards who glared at them from corner towers.

They turned a corner and moved out of sight of the prison fence.

"Good morning, Daniel." The blue suit shifted his attaché case and offered his free hand in greeting. "I am Mr. Chuma. Davison Chuma. Your father-in-law sent me to help."

Daniel heaved a sigh of relief. "Yes. Thank you. I've heard the name."

"I am glad you are well. Forgive me, but I must ask." Chuma leaned closer. "Inside the jail, did you hear of a man named Gideon Chipinduka?"

"The doctor?" Daniel nodded. "He is well."

"Praise God," Chuma said. They walked around another corner. A car door opened, a woman tumbled out and ran toward them.

"Sheila!" Daniel caught her, held her hard, arms fighting against the fear of it being a dream.

Chuma eyed the street and put his hand on Daniel's shoulder. "We must go. It is not safe here."

Chapter 15
Harare Prison, Zimbabwe

The guard slipped the cigarettes into a pocket and nodded to the watchers in the tower. His eyes followed the two men leaving the prison.

Knots of prisoners under the supervision of another guard trickled out on the far side of the yard. Now was his chance. He retraced his steps through the courtyard and stopped outside Gideon's door. He pulled the pack of cigarettes from his pocket.

Gideon watched from his cell, arms draped across metal bars. Ribs pressed determinedly against black skin.

"You want a smoke?" the guard asked.

"How many do you have left?" Gideon asked.

Without looking into the box, the man replied, "Only one."

Gideon nodded. "Yes. One is good."

The guard left, leaving Gideon alone.

Gideon turned away from the bars. Eyes white against the room's shadows. Just one, he thought. One more day.

Chapter 16
Harare Slum, Zimbabwe

A bat dripped from under a corrugated roof and flitted across the purple dusk. Mud brick and cinderblock shanties lined an alley that served as gutter, sewer and road. Davison Chuma avoided deep trenches the rain had cut between hopeless chunks of asphalt. Chuma stopped when he saw four men sitting with feet toward a fire, black faces bathed in orange. Chuma listened to the melody of their conversation and called softly to them.

He moved into the light and shook hands with each man in turn. A man named Darius gave Chuma his stool and settled himself on a grass mat. Davison sat down and they fell silent—listening to the night sounds. In the distance, a pop of gunfire set off a round of barking dogs. Indistinct music from a nightclub ebbed and flowed across the roofs of the shanty town. There, people gathered under inconsistent light bulbs to drink cheap beer, dance to the sound of tinny speakers, and get HIV.

"Baba, how is your family?" Chuma asked.

The grey headed man leaned forward and pulled a lighted twig from the fire. The glow fell into the wrinkles on his face as he lit a gourd pipe, turning his silver beard a momentary gold. "My family is well. The rains are good this year." He sucked in sallow cheeks, sent the smoke out through his nose and handed the round-bellied pipe to another. "My brother says there will be an extra ten bags of ground maize for market, or if demand is low, lots of extra beer."

The men chuckled, and the man continued, "He says there is no petrol, so he can only take the bags one by one to the market on his bicycle or sell them by the roadside. But there are no cars driving up and down the road. Even thieves who bribe truckers to sell diesel from their tanks have no business. Instead their yellow jerry tins sit empty. Now the village women use them to sell mangos." He gave a snort of disapproval and took up the pipe which had made its circle.

"Even thieves are going hungry," Darius said.

"Darius is right, but at least there are mangos." The old man's watery eyes squinted through the smoke. "And how is your family, Chuma?"

"My mother is well and my sister's husband is in town." Chuma would not use Gideon's name.

There were several surprised grunts from the circle. The old man pulled the pipe away from his mouth and stared long at Chuma. "Your late sister's husband?"

Chuma looked at the ground. Nodded.

"Is he well?"

Chuma stared into the glowing embers. "He is in school."

"School?" The grey beard turned to one of the men next to him, discussing this new development in Shona. Then he switched back to Gwembe. "I see. He has always been a scholar."

A chuckle of agreement floated around the fire. Chuma drew on the pipe and passed it to a man whose flip-flops had blown out on one side. Fine copper wire glinted in the firelight where the strap had been carefully stitched back together. Flip-Flop coughed a little as the bitter smoke tingled. His worn, green coveralls gaped open at the front. "Is it time to arrange a holiday for the student?"

Chuma replied. "Yes. I have made the arrangements. A friend has agreed to help transport him for the holiday."

"That is good," said the old man. He turned and addressed the younger three. "You will go to meet him?"

The three nodded. Silent. Solemn.

Chuma dropped his voice and continued, "We will meet by the Tires and Wires kiosk when the moon stands free of the horizon. The kiosk stands only a few hundred meters from the school gate where we will enter, just around the nearest corner. I have already informed my contact inside. When the guard in the tower climbs down, we create our diversion and enter through the main gate." Chuma removed his glasses, pulled a worn hanky from his suit pocket and wiped his face down thoroughly, trying to remove the stress. "We will have to move quickly. This may be our last chance. I hope we are not already too late." Chuma looked into the night sky. "Let us pray."

Chapter 17
Peacock Farm, Zimbabwe

Daniel lathered himself with soap for a third time. He stood under the shower for a long time and let hot water wash the filth from his body and tried to erase the smell from his memory. He wrapped the towel about his waist and stepped into the bedroom.

Stuart and Kathy had given Daniel and Sheila the guesthouse, knowing they needed some time together after the ordeal. It was a quaint affair, set on the banks of a pond Stuart used to irrigate his fields. The tiny porch was just large enough for two chairs where they could sit and have a sundowner. And it was safe.

Evening orange light spilled in through the door. A table for two, tucked into a corner, was covered with white linen, a plate of cold venison and hard boiled eggs. A bottle of bubbly nestled in an ice bucket. Sheila walked up behind Daniel and reached around him.

"I missed you so much," she purred. He turned, picked her up, and carried her to bed. He could feel her trembling.

"I was so afraid." Tears wet her dark lashes.

"I know." He rocked her gently, cradling her in his arms like a child.

#

She woke him after midnight. Pulled him close. His body woke first, hungry at the taste of skin, intoxicated by her fragrance. Tears mingled with desire and the scent of rain. Intermittent lightning broke the darkness, but they managed well enough by feel.

Afterward, they lay sweating under the mosquito net and listened to thunder retreating in the distance. Cool breeze played over hot skin.

After a time, Daniel broke the silence. "I have something to do tomorrow," he waited for her question then continued. "There was a man in prison with me. Chuma says he is the man who should be running the country. I think Chuma's right. But then, anyone would be better than what we've got. I am going to help him get out."

Sheila turned to him. "What are you talking about, Daniel? What are you planning?"

"A friend has arranged for his release from the prison, and I told him I would be on hand to make sure everything goes smoothly."

"You're joking right? You just got away from that hellhole, and you plan to go marching right back in there and make nice-nice with those bastards?"

"I'm not exactly going to be sitting down for tea with the guards. Our approach is a little more direct."

"I can't believe this. My life has been a living hell, wondering what they were doing to you. I didn't know where they had taken you." She sat up in bed. "I didn't even know if you were alive. Now you're telling me you're just going to run off again to visit that prison after hours, and I'm supposed to be okay with that? What do you want? Me to give you a kiss on the cheek and tell you to have a nice time with the boys?" Her voice rose with exasperation. "Now you *are* going to do something to get locked up for. I don't want to go through that again."

"Sheila, this is something I have to do. I'll be home before midnight. Your folks plan to leave around one a.m. I'll be back by then for sure."

Daniel touched her, but she pulled away. He got up. A thin moonlight covered his body as he looked into the darkness, the muscles of his jaw working. "I remember when I was a kid, my father used to say, 'If there is a snake in your garden, you must kill it.'"

"This is not your garden anymore," she said. "They don't want you here. They don't want me here." Her words were bitter and short. "And I don't want to be here either. I will not hang around a country where they can come and lock up your family just so they can get what they want."

He didn't answer. For a long time he stood there. He watched until the eastern sky began to lighten.

#

In the morning they met Sheila's parents in the garden of the main house for breakfast. They opted to eat outside, as their conversation would be more private.

"We will meet Chuma's contact at Mana Pools before daylight tomorrow morning." Stuart picked at his sausage and eggs without conviction. "Kathy and I think it would be safer if you came with us. As long as you are here, they will use you to try to get to us.

60

There is always the chance that whoever moves in here won't think about trying to obtain a legal title. But if they do, then it could get difficult for you," he paused and put his hand on Sheila's arm. "I am sorry. I wish you had not been drawn into this."

"Sheila and I have already talked about it," Daniel replied. He wiped his mouth on the serviette and picked up his teacup. "We need to run to our house in Harare and pick up a few necessaries."

"Do you think that is a good idea?" Kathy asked. "Who knows what will be waiting for you. Maybe you should go alone, Daniel."

"I'm going, mum." Sheila was adamant. "I want to see my home and get a few things before we leave. All our pictures are there. Everything." Sheila pushed a curl behind her ear and stared at her mother. "If I don't go, I will always regret it."

Daniel drained his tea. "We'll be back before lunch, mum." He looked at Stuart. "Would you mind if I used the Peugeot?"

"Yes, I'll need it this afternoon for a little errand, but you'll be back by then," Stuart replied.

Kathy rang the bell and Suzie appeared from the kitchen to clear the table.

Today was Suzie's first day back since the family funeral, and they had been able to do a little light packing in their rooms without raising too many questions. Almost everything would be left behind anyway.

As of yet, only Dodson, the stock manager, knew they planned to leave. They would make the announcement at noon. Too late to say goodbye properly. Too late to alert the government.

Stuart Hall spent most of the afternoon scuttling farm machinery. He could never get it across the border. He removed spark plug wires or battery cables, wrapped them carefully in oilcloth and packed the bundles into an empty grease drum. Then he hammered the edges of the lid down around the can until it was tightly sealed. When a country begins to die, as Zimbabwe had, spare parts become almost impossible to buy. Even if someone was able to figure out what was missing, they would be hard pressed to find a replacement anywhere in the country.

When the hired help left for the day, Stuart lifted the drum into the trunk of the Peugeot and grabbed a shovel. Wind blew in through the open windows as he picked his way through the fields, listening to the suspension rattling over the rough lane. The track cut between a meadow and the stock dipping tank. He walked the gate open, drove behind an outcropping of rock and pulled to a stop.

The shovel cut neatly into brown earth near the rock base. Smoke from cook fires at the workers' compound brought back memories that made his eyes water. His rough hands shook with adrenaline and sadness. He rolled the barrel into its grave. The dented drum held the last glimmering shard of hope, and he buried it in the ground. Stuart wiped the sweat and tears with the back of his hand and stamped down the dirt. When it rained again, the spot would be invisible. It was the best he could do. If Mwanyisa died, they might come back home. If the tractors were still there, they could restart the farm.

If.

Stuart returned to the main house by way of the workers' compound. The mud-brick houses with thatched roofs faced a common center. Several scrawny-necked chickens patrolled the bare earth, scuttling after grasshoppers.

Families cooked meals outside or under a round thatched pavilion when it rained. Most cooked over wood fires. Their braziers needed charcoal and that had been sold in town. Dodson, the stock manager and headman of the workers' village, got up from the shade and came to meet Stuart.

The headman's face hung in wrinkles. His bare feet splayed wide. The trousers he wore belonged to Stuart until Christmas time some-years back. Now they were patched and worn. Stuart smiled. The man had better clothes, but the trousers were a shared joke because Stuart had outgrown them around the middle.

Dodson shook Stuart's calloused hand and led him to the shade. They leaned their backs against earthy bricks and waited in the silence shared when someone dies. No wasted, empty words—just the quiet comfort of those who keep watch during the first hours of grief.

News that Stuart and Kathy were leaving the country spread quickly through the workers' compound. Though the Halls said they were leaving on Friday, they had to leave that night in order to meet Chuma's man near Mana Pools in the north.

"My friend, you know why we must leave."

"Yes." The old man nodded his head once, his yellowed eyes averted to show his sadness.

"I am flattered that the honorable Mwanyisa wants to buy my farm." Stuart looked out at the children playing in the clearing. The laughter of their football game seemed innocent and ignorant of the times. "I do not know what will happen to your families."

"Yes." Dodson's simple response belied the depth of his understanding. Including their dependents, Stuart and Kathy's business supported more than seventy-five people. It used to be many more, but the economy and the constant threat of the Land Reform Program had forced the Halls to scale back. For months they had only run a skeleton crew.

"You will look after the cattle?" Stuart got up to leave and placed his hand on the old man's shoulder. "They are yours now."

Dodson looked up at him, surprised. "Ndatenda."

Dodson accompanied Stuart out of the compound. The escort a sign hospitality. They stood by the hedgerow of sisal cacti that marked the edge of the compound, looking at the fields around them. How to say goodbye?

Stuart turned and embraced the man before driving back. He did not bother to wipe the tears that ran down his face.

The other workers had been sent home early with gifts of clothing and hand tools. Kathy gave Suzie several pots and pans before Suzie went home. They had stood together, crying in the kitchen. By the time the evening light faded, the Hall's single suitcase sat packed and ready by the front door.

Chapter 18
Harare Prison, Zimbabwe

The broken glass of a burnt out street light stared blankly at the kiosk below.

Bold black letters scrawled over the storefront's gaudy aqua blue paint read, 'Tyres and Wires Kiosk.' The life of the city around the prison continued on as if it were not there. Tyres and Wires was just another kiosk set up to make business in a country where every little bit helped.

The battered affair perched on the roadside like a vagrant with no real home. The foundationless cinderblock walls bulged and bellied in places and the front vaguely resembled a bank teller's window. The proprietor fashioned tire rubber into something like shoes and traded these for whatever he could get. Cash hadn't been used as a medium of exchange since Mwanyisa had leeched the economy into a coma.

Only three intact tires remained, leaning against the back wall of the kiosk. Inside, Chuma stared at four faces breathing in the darkness. Darius had a machete tucked through his belt, but Daniel held the only firearm. Darius and Flip-Flop wore no shoes, preferring the speed and silence of bare feet. They were an unlikely bunch of men to trust with the future of a nation, and Chuma tried not to think about what could go wrong.

Mwanyisa's arrogance caused him to be more lax than he should with some of his leading political opponents. From the jail, Gideon Chipinduka still managed to exert his influence through more indirect means. Gideon had secret contacts that extended into the royal palace. They would not be lucky for long. Soon Gideon would be moved to another prison, and, somewhere along the way, he would go 'missing' in transfer. Mwanyisa may be arrogant, but he held grudges to the death.

Chuma peered through a crack in the wall and studied the sky. No one would have guessed this man was an attorney who had been a player in the country's highest courts. He wore over-washed, sun-faded black trousers and shirt, both dark enough to match the night.

"We go now," Chuma said.

Flip-Flop moved first. He stepped out of the shack carrying a whiskey bottle almost full of petrol. When he neared the far corner of the prison grounds, Flip-Flop began to sing the national anthem. It sounded perfectly horrible. At another time, Chuma would have smiled. Flip-Flop's high tenor. Brazenly off key. Words mocking reality. "Oh lift the banner high, the flag of Zimbabwe, the symbol of freedom proclaiming victory."

Flip-Flop staggered along, singing louder and louder, pausing now and again to gain his balance, holding the bottle high as if in a toast to the men stationed in their watchtowers at the corner of the gate. He skirted the front of the prison compound and turned up the street that marked the far boundary. The men hiding in Tyres and Wires listened to the singing get farther away.

Flip-Flop could feel the guards watching. When he paused, pretending to sip from the flask, he could hear their laughter above him in the dark. His show broke the tedium of their watch. None seemed concerned. Flip-Flop belted out the words. Somewhere inside the prison block Gideon could hear the song and would be making himself ready.

The other men slipped from the kiosk. Chuma worked the wire cutters, popping his way through the fence, shielded from the guards compound by the actual prison block itself. Darius crouched beside him, studying the darkness.

Daniel remained in the kiosk. He worked open a hole in the side wall large enough to slide his rifle barrel through to provide back-up should the men run into trouble. But the hunting rifle was designed for accurate shots, not combat.

Chuma cut an inverted 'L' allowing them to peel the wire back forming a triangular opening. No time for more. Chuma darted through and went to work on the inside fence. He forced his eyes to focus on the wire, cutting the chain link one clip at a time, trusting Darius to watch for guards. This was no time to get distracted.

Flip-Flop dallied near the prison's far gate. A tire lay in the uneven, grassy bank of a drainage ditch. The guards did nothing. Flip-Flop was just another passer-by, though one who had the good fortune of being drunk-happy.

Flip-Flop lowered the bottle and emptied the contents into the rimless tire's cavity. He pitched the bottle into the ditch and pulled out a hand rolled cigarette. He let out another burst of song and lit the cigarette. Standing as close as he dared, Flip-Flop flicked the still burning match from his fingers.

The petrol bomb erupted in a blaze of fire and thunder that shook the ground. The tire lifted completely into the air and rolled burning into the ditch, spreading blazing gasoline as it went. Flip-Flop had started sprinting the moment he flicked the match and disappeared into the deeper shadows across the street. Guards scrambled to the scene, looking for action, firing off a few rounds just for fun.

Darius hissed and Chuma dropped, flattening himself against the ground. A man spilled from the warden's office, zipping up his trousers as he ran toward the commotion of fire, shouting soldiers and the pop of machine gun fire.

"Okay," Darius said and Chuma went to work again, fighting to make the clip-clip rhythm faster.

When the guard nearest the kiosk left his tower and joined the excitement, Chuma and Darius scrambled quickly through the openings in the fences.

Flip-Flop sprinted the perimeter of the prison facility, careful to stay in the shadows, glad for the blaze which compromised the soldiers' night vision. He climbed in the cab of a 1976 Landrover Discovery and turned the ignition. The engine sputtered to life. Flip-Flop wrestled the transmission into gear. With rpm's low and lights off, he continued around the prison block, coming full circle so the kiosk and main gate were ahead of him. Flip-Flop engaged the clutch and waited.

Chuma and Darius sprinted across the parade ground toward the warden's office. They burst through and pulled the door shut behind them.

A woman sat up from a low iron bed, holding a blanket to cover her nakedness. A single candle on the desk illuminated soft black skin. She ignored the machete and exchanged a few quick words with Chuma before handing over a ring of keys that sparkled even in the faint light.

Darius fought an old pair of handcuffs from his pocket and bound the woman's foot to the bed frame. Chuma took a razor from a folded paper in his pocket. He apologized to the woman before drawing the blade across her upper arm. She drew in a breath sharply, but made no other sound. They hoped the cut would keep her from being questioned.

Chuma rested his hand on her head and nodded his thanks.

The two men left the warden's room and disappeared into the prison. All along the way, prisoners called softly for release. Chuma ran just ahead of Darius until they reached Gideon's cell. The reek of filth and human sweat stung their noses. The erratic light from Flip-Flop's fire outside played weird shadows across the cells in Gideon's hall.

Gideon Chipinduka's hands reached through the bars and took the wad of keys. Every cell had its own unique padlock, another indicator that the prison had been cobbled together from the rubble of a once prosperous society. Black hands returned holding the correct key apart from the others. Chuma opened the lock and the three fled back the way they had come. Before they left the hall, Chuma handed the raft of keys to a single outstretched hand extending from the cell nearest the warden's office.

Darius peered out of the warden's door and motioned for the others to exit. Chuma and Gideon pressed themselves against the outside wall until Darius joined them. With Gideon in the middle, the men fled back across the open parade ground toward the fence.

Behind them came the staccato popping of automatic gunfire. The ground exploded. Bullets sprayed wide and to the right. They drove on toward the opening, willing legs to move faster. Ahead of them, light flashed as Daniel returned fire from the kiosk.

They flung themselves on the first rough opening, fingers pulling on fence, labored breathing, they pushed each other through—bare wire clinging to clothing, scratching their sides. Guns rattled and bullets smacked the dirt close behind as they scrambled across no-man's land between the fences. They forced Gideon first through the final opening. Chuma followed, rolling down into the cover of the drainage ditch. Darius shirt snagged on the fence. Gunfire tattered overhead, splattering against the cinderblock wall, guards still shooting blindly into the shadows. Darius tumbled, shirtless, into the ditch.

Blood pulsed from a hole in his chest, ran down his stomach and stained the grass. In the near dark, the blood looked black.

Flip-Flop pulled the Landrover past the kiosk. Daniel sprinted from the shack and leapt into the rear of the vehicle which then roared toward the point of intersect with the three men. Flip-Flop threw the stick into neutral, and Daniel slipped out and helped Chuma and Gideon lift Darius into the vehicle. Flip-Flop popped the clutch and sped away.

In the middle of the chaos and fire, several other black shadows fled the compound, climbing over wires that tore their flesh and stole pieces of clothing.

Darius's machete lay next to the playground, but it didn't matter.

He wouldn't need it anymore.

Chapter 19
Mana Pools National Park, Zimbabwe

The Rat sat under the wing of his airplane. The far-away sound of a lion's roar carried through the night. He slapped absently at a mosquito and re-lit his cigar, hoping to keep the mosquitoes at bay. "Damn pests," he muttered.

The grunting calls of hippos echoed up and down the Zambezi. They clambered up the bank to graze near the grassy runway. Strange creatures. Once out of the water, they became intolerably insecure, panicked easily and would run over whatever blocked their retreat to water. 7,000 pounds of hippo could make a sizeable impression on a plane.

The Rat heard the whine of a vehicle's engine. In the bush, sound traveled far and he knew his passengers could still be almost thirty minutes away, winding their way through the foothills of the escarpment.

Everyone called him The Rat, but the airplane title showed one Joey Greer. Portugal originally commissioned the FTB 337G Cessna Skymasters, but several found their way into service for the Royal Rhodesian Air Force. After the war in Zimbabwe ended, some of the twin boom, push-pull airplanes were decommissioned and sold privately. Though The Rat's Skymaster carried a Zambian registration, it frequently found its way into surrounding countries. He'd flown into Mozambique, but frequented mining camps in the Democratic Republic of Congo. Several expatriate workers there had enough money to avoid the unreliable local infrastructure on weekends.

The Rat charged a premium for countries he deemed unstable and, consequently, made a sweet profit for flights into the DRC. The Rat specialized in hot zones, and the clientele he attracted paid handsomely for his services.

Joey, The Rat, would fly for just about any cause, so long as it included money. And money brought him to Mana Pools. An email confirmed a wire transfer into his bank in Sweden.

That was all he needed to know.

Mana Pools covered almost 800 square miles along the Zambezi River and up to the escarpment in the south. It boasted some of the finest wildlife and least developed wild places on the continent.

He scratched his unshaven face and stowed the folding chair in the Cessna's cargo pod. The kind of people who flew with him expected to leave on time.

The Rat switched on a flash light and began his pre-flight. From wildlife to militants, normal conditions didn't exist in his world. He opened the fuel caps and did a visual check topside. Then he pushed the fuel tester onto the valve beneath the tanks, drawing off moisture and debris until the tester pulled a clear draft.

He scanned the runway again. The hippos had moved off.

Within a few minutes, The Rat could see the vehicle's headlights cut through the bush as it pulled out onto the flood pan. It parked at the rear of the airstrip. Three men and two women exited the car and worked quickly to unload their few possessions. Fifteen kilograms each was the limit he had set.

The Rat pulled two flares from the cargo pod and strode toward the far end of the runway. A night takeoff with no ground lights and possible hippos put most pilots on the potty. He paced off 300 meters, pulled the flare caps and struck the scratch surface across the igniter button. White fire hissed from the end of the orange sticks. He positioned them on either side of the grassy lane and jogged back to the plane, hoping nothing else trespassed on his runway.

The five travelers stood dumbly around the plane while he wrestled the baggage into the pod.

"You're bleary lucky we don't have any hippos tonight, eh?" he said by way of greeting. "We'll put you ladies in the back seats." He flashed his light on Sheila and Kathy. "I don't want to be distracted," he said with a wink which they couldn't see in the dark. "You two," He pointed at Stuart and Daniel, "ride behind me." He put his hand on Gideon's shoulder, "and you can ride next to me. Danny says you're like a reverend or something, and God knows we might need some of His help tonight, eh?" The Rat laughed and helped them get inside and find their seatbelts.

The roar of twin propellers engulfed the silence. He threw on landing lights and finished his pre-flight check.

He crossed himself and turned to Gideon. "You pray; I drive. Alright?"

Gideon nodded, but his eyes were wide.

The plane bumped down the runway, gaining speed over the rough ground, heading toward the blazing flares. Finally, the nose lifted, and they were airborne.

Chapter 20
Mazabuka, Zambia

Chuma traveled from Harare to Lusaka on a commercial flight to manage the necessary clearances for the two families in Zambia. Since arriving, he had spent much time talking with Stuart and Daniel. The families decided to settle in Mazabuka, just two hours south of the capital, but they had contrived another meeting with Chuma.

He disembarked from the crowded bus. The healthy activity in and around Mazabuka reminded him of what Zimbabwe had once been. Chuma purchased a roasted mealies from a woman who set up her brazier beside the bus stop and began picking off the hot kernels one at a time. He had not eaten since that morning—save for a biscuit and tea in one of the government offices. Still he found himself refreshed to be in a country where business was possible, and one could deal with government offices without fear.

Of course, he paid significant bribes in order to have the necessary paperwork expedited. But this was not unexpected, and Stuart had given him enough cash to make sure there were no problems.

The pieces of Chuma's grand puzzle fell into place.

He turned down a dirt road cut between huge fields of sugar cane. Many of these fields had once been under contract with the Zambian Royal Sugar Company.

Most of the large land holders were white Zambians, farmers born and raised here. A few had immigrated from Zimbabwe and South Africa, the latter coming in droves after the fall of apartheid. The

Zambian government soon realized the cultural and political ramifications and began to clamp down. While this served to keep out those who might come with a racial bias, it also kept out farmers who would bring the means to develop large-scale agricultural schemes and the jobs to go with them. Chuma walked around to the back of a farmhouse.

A stone patio extending off the back of Patrick Boll's house overlooked a grassy lawn. A group of men stood around holding drinks. Chuma thought they looked more like rugby players gathered for a post-game celebration, but the mood was somber. Besides Stuart and Daniel, there were three other men, all of them white, Zimbabwean farmers in exile.

"Davison. There you are." Stuart walked over to him. "Fantastic to see you." He embraced his friend. "Looks like you have started quite a fire here," he said soberly. Stuart turned to the others. "Gentlemen, this is Chuma, Davison Chuma. He is the attorney who orchestrated our exodus from Zimbabwe. Not only that, but he was solely responsible for getting Daniel out of jail and organizing the removal of Gideon Chipinduka from right under the nose of the old tyrant himself."

Daniel stepped forward and handed a drink to Chuma. Then he raised his bottle in a toast. "To Chuma." Glass clinked around him as he continued. "Here in Zambia it is easy to forget. Look around you," Daniel's eyes took in the sweep of the horizon. "It's all so familiar to us and yet somehow so different. Just a few hours south, there are people who every single day live with a different reality. They have no jobs. The money is a joke. They are lucky to find enough to eat. You are here because you decided to do something more than grumble about how you lost your farm or your business or your home. Thank you for coming. I don't have to tell you how important this is."

Stuart continued. "Gideon Chipinduka could not be with us tonight as he has to remain in hiding. It is our job to see that he gets safely home." Stuart motioned to the other men. "Chuma, this is Aaron Boll and his father Patrick. That old buzzard is Howard Cambric."

The white haired man stepped forward and shook Chuma's hand. "Yes. Cambric, like the tea."

The men moved to a teakwood patio table and sat down. Chuma began the meeting with prayer. Aaron Boll, sitting to Daniel's left, held his cigarette underneath the table so God wouldn't notice. Chuma began in English and ended in Shona, his words soft and urgent.

When he had finished, Aaron asked, "So how do you know God is on our side?" He was smiling, but his question was serious.

"God hates injustice," Chuma replied. "It has always been this way, but a man named Deitrich Bonhoeffer also asked this question. For him the problem was not Mwanyisa, it was Hitler. In the end Bonhoeffer decided he could not stand before God knowing he had done nothing. He said, 'Leaders and offices which set themselves up as gods, mock God and must perish.' So he made a plan to assassinate Hitler."

"I guess we know how that went," Aaron said wryly.

"Yes. He failed." Chuma conceded. "But when we stand against injustice, we stand with God. You are able to leave the country because you have money, and I have contacts. But my people, our people, are not so free. They have to remain and wonder where they are going to find food. They have to wonder which of them will starve. The rest of the world has forgotten about Zimbabwe. And, perhaps, our people are wondering if God has forgotten about Zimbabwe as well."

"And what makes you think we'll be successful if Bonhoeffer wasn't?" Aaron leaned over and flicked cigarette ash into the ashtray.

"To take a stand for justice is to succeed. To do nothing is to fail. A wise man once said that all evil needs to triumph is for good men to do nothing?"

The men sat for a while in a kind of holy silence as the gravity of what they were doing began to sink in. Though all of them knew how to handle firearms and were capable trackers, only Stuart had seen any kind of military combat. But they had all lost something under Mwanyisa's regime.

"While we all hope Heaven follows us into our little battle," Stuart picked up from Chuma, "it is our job to make sure that we have everything in order. Based on the information Chuma has given us, there will be a narrow window of opportunity within the next few weeks. The three of us," he pointed at Chuma and Daniel, "have come up with a plan which we'll share with you tonight. At least in part. Secrecy is paramount."

Stuart's prior training brought a comforting sense of leadership. Chuma's little speech had taken care of the ethical question and opened the way for them to take themselves seriously.

The men picked up their drinks to make a space, and Stuart rolled out a map.

Chapter 21
Mazabuka, Zambia

The two families moved into a partially furnished house in Mazabuka. It belonged to a Korean businessman who had left the country for a year, and Stuart managed to contact him via email to arrange the rental. The house had divided in-law quarters, joined by a single door, where Daniel and Sheila did their best to settle in after setting the requisite bombs for cockroaches and sweeping up the piles.

Sheila found a mosquito net at the local ShopRite and hung it from the hook. It would help to deter the more resilient roaches from exploring their bed and was even, in a way, romantic. Sheila had just begun to feel the letdown from the stress of the last week when Daniel returned from his meeting with Chuma and whispered his intentions.

"You don't give a shit about me," she said. "All you care about is your damn Africa. You are just like my father."

"Sheila—"

"Don't Sheila me. I swore I would never marry a man like him. I thought because you weren't interested in farming you might be different, but I was wrong." Her flushed face made the freckles stand out.

Daniel didn't try to touch her. She sat down on the edge of their bed and ignored the hot angry tears. He knew she was in shock.

"I have to do this thing." His words were apologetic. "I don't have anything to give you. All of my dreams included you and Zimbabwe. I'm not willing to give up on that yet."

"Choose." Tears continued to roll down her face, sobbing fiercely controlled. "Choose one."

Daniel walked to her. "What are you saying?"

"If you are going to pick Zimbabwe, then I'm leaving. It is one or the other."

"You are asking me to stop caring. I care about you. I care about Africa."

"I'm leaving," she said softly. "Tomorrow. I'll be going away for a while."

Daniel put his hand on the side of her face and pushed a curl behind her ear. He let his hand rest there. "Then I will come find you." There was nothing else he could say. He opened the door and stepped into the night.

Sheila sat there, stunned. Couldn't believe it was over so soon. It wasn't supposed to end this way. He was supposed to scoop her up, take her to bed, make love to her and promise never to leave. She wrapped her arms around herself and whispered after him, "Please don't die."

Chapter 22
Kariba Dam, Zambia

Earlier that morning, Gritson Chalwanda had given Wolfe's paperwork a cursory glance and decided it wasn't worth his effort to hassle the man. The customs agent vaguely remembered an official notice from his superiors in Lusaka explaining that a borehole was going to be drilled behind the border-crossing station.

The border between Zambia and Zimbabwe was quiet. The traffic that passed between the two countries was mostly local tourists on day trips. The customs official contented himself with searching the luggage of those he deemed a threat to national security, usually rich men and beautiful women. In between these 'threats', Gritson Chalwanda moved out of the building and sat under the breezy shade of the mango tree. Here he was free of the watchful eyes of his honorable president whose obligatory photograph hung behind the customs counter.

Gritson Chalwanda was glad to have something to pass the time until he could officially go on lunch break. Nothing like boredom to make one hungry. He leaned up against the tree and sipped at a bottle of tepid soda. He wasn't sure why they needed another borehole, but he had long since stopped trying to make sense out of official government issues and instead was content to let life happen to him just the way it would.

Sean Wolfe watched as well from his vantage point on the opposing hill. He had glasses on the men from the moment the guard unlocked the padlocked fence and let his boys through. The shell and auger drilling rig maneuvered into the tight space.

The Consallen Forager 55/1250 required only two men to operate. Neither of them had met Wolfe. As far as they knew, someone in the government had contracted this job. The enticement had been the chance to travel to an out-of-the-way place where the women were cheaper. Decreased traffic drove down demand which drove down price. Economics were the same everywhere.

The operators disconnected the tow-behind unit and used the winch from the vehicle to stand the tripod rig over the flag Wolfe had placed to mark the spot. The trailer wheels rose off the ground as the winch whined, and the tongue of the trailer became one leg of the tripod. They arranged the pyramid shaped structure so the free falling cutter in the center would hit its mark exactly.

In spite of a drilling capacity of almost 500 feet, the rig seemed remarkably unpretentious. From Wolfe's vantage point it looked not unlike a naked teepee with a motor at its base. The powerhouse in this case was a 10-horse power Lister-Petter diesel boasting over twenty-two hundred pounds of hoisting strength. The drill worked on the same principle as a hand held post-hole digger. The rig's cable lifted the weighted cutting tool to the apex of the twenty-four foot frame and let it drop.

With various cutting tools and sinker bars, the rig would make rapid progress through the loamy soil until they hit bedrock. At that point they would continue on a few feet before inserting the shell casings to keep the sides from collapsing. Then they would install a temporary cap. The boys today would be drilling a single 6 inch bore, stopping at exactly 414 feet below the surface of the ground.

This depth would provide the perfect leverage point. The hole would be the fulcrum upon which Esposito's entire back-up plan would hinge.

The two workers began drilling as soon as the rig had been fully assembled. Wolfe could not hear the sound of the diesel engine but every now and then, he heard the clang of steel as the assistant hammered out a recalcitrant cotter pin in order to attach a different cutter drill.

According to their instructions, they would inform the border agent that a man from the company would come later to inspect their work.

Chapter 23
Lusaka, Zambia

Howard Cambric cut an unlikely ally in a scheme to assassinate a president. He looked more like an eccentric scientist and was, in fact an amateur lepidopterist. His collection held almost 700 species representing the Ethiopian faunal region, which included most of the African continent. The teak and glass butterfly cases now hung on display in a private museum in England. Cambric's untidy, white eyebrows and sharp nose surrounded intense eyes. He had the mind of a chess player and, as a result, Stuart Hall tasked Cambric with sourcing anything the boys might need for their mission.

The motorcycles he purchased used from a vendor in South Africa. Patrick Boll, who assisted Cambric with logistics, would pick up the bikes in Johannesburg and transport them to Zambia on his trailer. Patrick Boll would, of course, be traveling through Botswana because any quantity of fuel was impossible to find in Zimbabwe. Patrick would get the bikes tuned up and ready to roll.

The sniper rifles proved more complicated. Cambric knew they needed to get the weapons as soon as possible. The nations of the Southern African Development Community would soon be convening in Lusaka. They had to be ready.

Cambric picked at his eyebrows, his face reflecting the computer's blue screen. He had set up an account under a bogus business name through one of his contacts in New Zealand. Working via a proxy site, Howard Cambric made contact with a munitions broker in Canada. According to the website, the man lived near Toronto, but Cambric didn't care so long as the man could deliver. His reviewers claimed the broker shipped on time, every time. And time was important.

The withdrawal came at exactly 8:03am Eastern Standard Time. Cambric watched online as the charge for three, identical SSG 08's showed up in his ledger.

#

The broker wondered that sniper rifles ordered by a New Zealand registered Safari outfit were an odd choice for wild game, but hunters were particular about their firearms and the money was real enough. At $5,400 USD a piece, who was he to argue?

The weapons had been easy to locate. A regional gun show ran a special on the Steyr Mannlicher, which certainly didn't hurt his bottom line. The Steyr Scharf Shutzen Gewehrifle had a good reputation among military and police sniper units in Austria and was being marketed to the US Armed Forces as well.

The broker simply packed the rifles with the required supply of .308 cartridges and declared them 'farm machinery' on the bill of lading. After all, he reasoned, one does need to keep down pests on a farm. The buyer wanted the weapons shipped to a customs agent in Zambia. His customers had been in a terrible hurry, and hurry was expensive. Not a bad gig for a month's salary.

#

The rifles arrived in Lusaka on Monday, two weeks prior to the SADC convention. The customs agent received a generous donation from an unnamed source and he found himself suddenly eager to expedite clearance. His willing participation, he had been told, would result in another bonus. He stamped the import documents and daydreamed about how to spend his money.

Stuart arranged for Aaron Boll to make the pick-up in Lusaka. Daniel, Stuart and Aaron, the shooters, planned to leave Mazabuka as soon as the units arrived for some practice in the bush.

Aaron lifted the package, slid it onto the bed of his Fiat pick-up, and closed the tailgate. He signed the last of the paperwork and returned the battered clipboard to the clearance agent.

Aaron would return to Mazabuka with the package in plain sight. The team had discussed this at length and in the end determined their best defense against curiosity was merely to put the boxes in full view of the military police who manned the various check points he would have to pass. Aaron also made the most frequent trips to Lusaka for business and was most likely to be recognized by the police, thereby further decreasing the likelihood of questions or delays.

Chapter 24
Presidential Palace
Harare, Zimbabwe

Cedric Mwanyisa stood in the center of his reading room and admired the furnishings. His favorite leopard skin rug sat before an ebony-carved, high-back chair that had been upholstered in London by the same upholster who worked for the royal family. Bookshelves extended from floor to ceiling in that corner and the window looked out on a garden stolen from a painting by Monet. Near the reading chair, a three-legged pie table held a silver tea set with gold filigree. Service for one.

Mwanyisa sighed contentedly and picked his teeth with an ivory toothpick. His selection of reading material ranged from early English poets to the political writings of colonial India, first prints of David Livingstone's work as well as signed copies of most of the early American poets. Though Mwanyisa had a grand library, he had long since left academic reading behind. He retained his library simply because of the way it made him feel—intelligent, powerful, and legitimate.

The legal volumes were housed in the library by his office, though he rarely had occasion to consult these works. He frequently reminded his advisors, 'In Zimbabwe, I am the law.'

The advisors had, at one time, been thinking creatures. Some even retained a sense of responsibility toward the people they represented. But the luster and enticement of wealth and power worked its magic and they, to a man, were transformed into a groveling consortium of sycophants. It paid to agree with the dictator. The advisors assisted the big man in managing affairs of state in such a way as to assure the highest profits and the least interference from political opposition or outside pressures.

Mwanyisa made a sour face. The presumption of outside nations rankled. To be directed as though he were a child of England or the United States put him in a foul mood, indeed.

Mwanyisa settled himself into a chair and put his feet on a zebra-skinned ottoman. He tried not to think about the Americans. A few renegade journalists had made some unfortunate contacts within the American media and it created unnecessary complications for those still involved in international trade agreements with his country. But the journalists would be dealt with.

Just today he had watched his internet surveillance system go live. The tech firm from Finland had been most helpful. Within a few minutes, the master computer began data groping, returning leads his security staff would follow. No subversion would be tolerated.

He would not allow other nations to interfere with his sovereign state. He would expose the errant political ambitions of those within his country who felt they could leverage their own agenda by linking hands with any government who would listen.

A gentle tap sounded at his door. Mwanyisa rarely entertained in his private sanctuary. Today, however, was an exception.

He rose from the chair and moved toward the library shelves.

"My friend, please come in." Behind him Banda entered and stood by the door, dwarfed into silence by the room's opulence. Across from the picture window an ornate fireplace mantle nestled between another matching pair of dark wood bookcases. The rosewood floor inlaid with American hickory gleamed beneath a domed ceiling. The dome supported a single chandelier—crystal and gold and imposing. "Thank you for coming to my private office." The dictator did not turn but continued to run his finger over the volumes. "Do you like to read?"

The younger man found his voice. "Yes, sir." Eyes wide with awe. "I like to read westerns."

Mwanyisa gave a short low chuckle. "And who is the author of these stories?" he asked.

"They are written by Louis L'Amour."

"Yes. I have heard of him. He is a Frenchman, is he not?" Mwanyisa inquired, waiting for the man to contradict him.

A brief hesitation before he answered, "Yes." Always agree with a dictator.

"I also like stories of war." Mwanyisa pulled a canvas cover carefully bound over pages brown with age. He turned to his visitor. "This is a history of Shaka Zulu." The man stood rooted, nodding dumbly. Mwanyisa continued, held the book out to his visitor. "Unlike your westerns, this is written by an American scholar."

Mwanyisa watched Banda begin to tremble. This was proving to be an interesting evening. He opened the book, flipping casually through the pages to find what he wanted. He walked to his chair and sat down. "Come and sit." Mwanyisa directed the man to the ottoman at his feet. Banda came quickly, being careful to stoop enough that his head was always lower than the dictator's.

"Shaka Zulu led one of Africa's finest armies. He would easily have defeated the white men had it not been for the Gatling gun."

Banda stared at the floor—head bobbing like some frightened schoolboy.

Mwanyisa continued. "He is a largely misunderstood figure in Africa's history. Those who have written about him determined he was a wicked and violent man. They do not like that he dealt decisively with any who opposed his rule. Yet because of this, Shaka Zulu was able to unite his people against a powerful neighbor. If he had not dealt quickly with those who failed him—even his friends—he would not have succeeded. Do you not agree?"

"Yes." Of course. The word barely audible.

"Perhaps you will find this interesting." Mwanyisa skimmed the page. "Ah yes, here it is." It tells of one unfortunate person who had made the mistake of losing one of Shaka's white bulls to a wild animal. Shaka had a stick sharpened in front of the man and then carefully planted the stick in the ground at the edge of his kraal." He handed the book to his advisor. "Read here."

Banda stared at the page. Took the book and read haltingly. "Then Shaka's men stripped the offender and lifted him screaming onto the sharpened stick so that he was impaled. At sundown, the man still moved, his incomprehensible groans bringing smiles to Shaka's face. Not wanting to fall asleep before seeing him die, Shaka ordered a small fire built under the man's feet." Banda swallowed hard and looked up. Beads of sweat formed on his forehead and Mwanyisa could see his trembling. He pointed at the book for Banda to continue.

"When the victim's wiggling finally stopped, Shaka retired to his bed chamber." Banda closed the book.

Mwanyisa shifted in his seat, aroused by the story of absolute power.

He continued from memory, "The next day Shaka repeated the process with the man's wives, contentedly eating his meals outside to watch as they writhed in agony around him."

Mwanyisa let silence hang in the room. Still, Banda said nothing.

"I think this Shaka was a good man." Mwanyisa returned the book to its place on the shelf then went to stand before his advisor whose trembling bulk dwarfed the ottoman. "How can I now be respected as a leader unless I also deal with those who have failed me?"

Mwanyisa put a hand on the man's shoulder, a tender gesture. "I am afraid, my friend, that you have failed me. I received word from those who are loyal, that one of my prisoners has escaped."

Banda said nothing. Eyes wide with horror, mesmerized by Mwanyisa's voice.

The dictator continued, "This prison was under your command."

The president's tone lightened. "Tonight I have ordered a fine veal. Why don't you join me? We will share a bottle of 1986 Montrachet. You have a long night ahead of you, and you will need all your strength."

Chapter 25
Pamodzi Hotel
Lusaka, Zambia

Colette Logan waited in the lobby of the Pamodzi Hotel in Lusaka. She held a tonic and watched yellow weaverbirds hanging upside-down from their nests in the courtyard. The overlay of accented conversations reminded her she was back in Africa.

Ciro Michi had called her in for this job. He said he needed someone he could trust, but nothing more. The other field operative would fill in the details. She didn't like to work blind, but the man paid well. Michi had his reasons for secrecy.

Colette's business often took her to various parts of the vast continent, and in some disturbing way, she always felt like she was coming home. Her own story began somewhere in South Africa at a time when a colored man had no business sharing a white woman's bed. Colette's mother had not seen it that way, and as a result, Colette wore a honey brown skin–the envy of any white woman looking for a tan.

Color was all her Indian father had given her. Not long after her birth, when the specifics of her paternity could no longer be hidden, several of Colette's uncles found the man, beat him with pieces of iron pipe, and dumped his body on the edge of one of Johannesburg's more violent townships. At that time, justice did not try as hard for men of color, and the murder went unresolved.

Her mother fled with Colette, first to Durban and then to England, where a woman with a colored child could live with less scrutiny. Her parents looked for them at first, but not very hard. The scandal of a colored child had a net loss in their social circles. It did not matter that the men in her family helped themselves to colored women in Johannesburg's brothels, whelping, in all likelihood, dozens of little brown crayons themselves.

It was the story of South Africa.

A different shame haunted them in England. The shrewd press of poverty further embittered her mother, who fought against it by working her own kind of revenge on her proper white family by doing everything she could to raise her precocious and intelligent, honey-colored daughter alone. But old age comes quickly for those in poverty. Long hours working jobs she never explained soon put the chances of finding a husband far out of reach. Still, her mother managed enough money to send Colette away to a respectable boarding school, which was just as well. A tired mother is no match for the cheddar sharp imp who was then almost thirteen.

Though the British schoolmasters managed to refine and polish the girl, they had been unable to break her spirit. By age sixteen, Colette moved to the top of her form, easily outdistancing her peers in languages. However, when her Latin teacher called her to his office after class, Colette discovered her true power.

He said he wanted to discuss a recent examination, but she found him more interested in slipping his hands underneath her clothing. She excused herself and ran.

Back in the dorm, she showered, tried to wash away the feel. Colette studied herself in the mirror, aware for the first time of a new and dangerous strength—a weapon she could use against men. It was a kind of victory for herself and her mother, who had, by then died quietly somewhere in the darker shadows of London.

Colette lay awake that night, certain that everything had changed.

The rest of the term, she practiced on her Latin teacher. While she never let him touch her again, she studied his every reaction, taking notes as feverishly as she had during any of his tedious lectures on the intricacies of the Latin tongue. Colette also studied in earnest the interactions of the couples around campus. Her obsession with cataloging the art of feminine power grew into several composition books. From her notes, she carefully planned every interaction with her Latin teacher—a man reported to be happily married with several children.

The professor, according to the Form 1 students, grew increasingly distracted, though none guessed the true reason. Just before the holidays, Colette put the final snare in place.

Three days before the end of term, Colette passed him a note with three simple words. *Write to me.*

It was the last step before extortion. While her lure had been simple enough, his response exceeded three pages, grossly specific and carefully signed in his own hand.

He had no idea what it would cost him.

The next day Colette dropped by the man's home before he returned from work, kindly introducing herself to his family. She explained how she was just out this way, and thought she would pop in and meet the woman he talked so much about in class. The wife, flattered if not a little surprised, invited her in.

The look on his face when he came home was priceless. He found them talking and sipping tea like a couple of old friends. Colette left a few minutes later, but not before gushing over the man's wife and kids.

The following morning he found a typewritten note with specific instructions and a bank routing number. He would have to make up his own cover story explaining the new expense to his wife. Perhaps some monthly contribution to a new charity. The last two lines of Colette's note read, *If your marriage falls apart, I'll give a copy of your kind letter to the academic dean. If you stop or miss payment, I'll give a copy to your wife. Lots of love, C.L.*

By the time she sat for the A Level examinations, Colette was receiving a tidy monthly income from four professors. All the men carefully chosen because they had many years before retirement, had families, and loved the accolades and respect they gained from their positions.

It had all been pathetically simple. Money for silence.

Colette finished the tonic and tapped the empty glass with her painted fingernails. The tiled hotel courtyard held a mélange of Zambian and international businessmen—not a bad place to go prospecting for new sources of income. In the last ten years, she refined her approach and purposely sought out men of significant wealth and power. That was how she found Ciro Michi, or he found her.

The Italian seemed like an easy target. His yacht hinted at obvious wealth and he appeared to have a wonderful relationship with his wife. They met in the Caribbean where Colette was studying for a deep water scuba certification.

Ciro Michi wasn't her first mistake, but he could easily have been her worst. It was the first time she had been caught in a con, and her first impulse was to run. She flirted and seduced, but he called her bluff, chuckled and handed her a martini. "Please have a seat, Colette."

The sound of her own name sucked the breath from her lungs. He motioned to the leather sofa that wrapped the top deck of his yacht. "Perhaps we can help each other."

No one had used her real name since she left school. She sat gasping, raw at the exposure. "What do you mean?" She bristled in the trap, but he seemed to have no intention of using her.

"I have been watching you for the past year." He clicked a remote. A monitor emerged from the paneled wall of his yacht. Pictures flashed across the screen of Colette in her own apartment, illustrating the stuff of daily life she thought was known to no one. The photography was clear and crisp—not what one would expect from a spy. The pictures documented her recent 'acquisitions', but then the record began to rewind. He had found almost every one of her men.

"There are doubtless others." Michi remarked with a shrug. His eyes an odd combination of kindness and cold. "I have seen your diaries. Interesting reading, but not the kind of thing you should leave laying around in safety deposit boxes. Still, I think I have managed to help you with a problem."

"I'm listening." Colette replied.

"Your journal lays out a specific plan to end the lives of your uncles, one Darwin Logan and another Frederick Logan. Gentlemen, I understand, responsible for the murder of your father. You seemed quite willing to write frankly about their death and even specified how they should be strangled slowly."

"You had no right to read that!" Colette suddenly angry.

"Now you have decided to worry about one's rights?" Michi shrugged. "You'll be happy to know both men have been taken care of in exactly the manner you proposed. Exactly. Of course, I had to make copies of your diaries, so I could attend to the specifics."

Michi flicked a few buttons on the remote and an image appeared of two men Colette recognized from family photographs. Only they were older, gray haired; their faces now twisted, purple and lifeless.

Seeing her own fantasies of revenge now so vividly presented before her filled her with excitement and a throbbing panic. Michi had no boundaries. All he had to do was send her journal to the South African authorities and she would be in a shit-load of trouble.

"Your approach is clean, uncomplicated, effective, and somewhat amateurish." Michi moved on. "You will soon need alternate identities. If you think your targets won't hire private investigators to find a way to shake you off their trail, then you are more naïve than I thought."

His words stung her pride, but Colette knew he was right.

"I am a wealthy man," Michi continued, "which you no doubt noticed before you decided to fall in love with me. My work, like yours, is of a kind that generates huge profits." Michi continued his presentation as if he were covering the logistics of a new marketing venture. "My business partners are never allowed to betray me. Never. If they do, I follow up. A relationship must be based on trust." He sipped water from a green glass bottle.

"What is your business?" Colette asked.

"That is not important. What is important is that there are times when I need to follow up, but I cannot be seen to be connected."

She nodded, but didn't understand. She knew nothing of the intricate and complicated world of Italian Mafia.

"I am not afraid to remove those who prove disloyal," Michi continued, "but sometimes the political ramifications within the family would get messy." He spread his hands and shrugged. Business as usual. "I need a wiseguy, an outside agent. Someone like you."

"Okay. And what if I say no? I haven't had much experience on the murder front," Colette admitted.

"You will not have to murder anyone, if you don't want to. Just put them in the right place. Besides, experience is not important. Talent is important. You have talent. I will train you." He leaned on the rail, the azure waters spread out before him. "And because you are self-employed, you do not have to take every job. I only require the strictest confidentiality." He turned and looked back at her. His hard eyes were deadly serious. "Money for silence."

That was *her* game. "I understand," Colette thought for a moment. She wasn't sure if he meant her silence, or his. "What do I get out of it?"

"Money. Experience. I will pay you, train you, and my contacts make it possible for you to travel anywhere. Alternate identities, paperwork, passports, banking, etc. No problem." Michi played hardball quid pro quo.

Colette needed an answer to the identity problem. Because of this limitation, she traveled broadly, never booking too many sources in one location. She put down her martini and said, "When do I start?"

Later she learned the scope and nature of Michi's business and counted herself lucky.

His offer of wealth and unlimited power over men had been intoxicating. The murder of her uncles left her feeling crudely trapped and, yet, somehow taken care of by the old man.

As promised, the pay was incredible.

The loneliness, however, she had not anticipated. It gnawed at the edges of her mind whenever she wasn't working a lead. The nature of her career choice kept her seeking new and more sophisticated men, and moving away from men who were already making monthly contributions.

When she wasn't working, she trained to keep her mind away from the loneliness. In the last ten years, she'd achieved a passable proficiency in three new languages. Under Michi's tutors, Colette studied Italian, skydiving and self-defense. The first two added to her aura as an exotic woman, the last a hedge against a time when she might find herself in a jam.

"Good morning." A greeting brought her back to reality. "You must be Colette, yes?" The voice startled her, but not nearly as much as the use of her real name. She smiled. A hint of an English accent. Clean cotton slacks below a blue shirt with a light blazer. No tie. No frumpy Englishman, here. His hands looked rough and strong.

"I am Sean Wolfe." He settled himself on the wicker. A waiter appeared and Wolfe ordered water with lemon. They sat together without speaking, watching the yellow birds hanging upside down from their nest.

Since her school days, no one had ever used her real name. No one except Ciro Michi. She would speak to him about this.

Chapter 26
Presidential Palace
Harare, Zimbabwe

Advisors gathered around the conference table, speculating quietly about the meeting. Unlike their countrymen, they all carried extra weight. Tailored suits, watches on gold chains, designer reading glasses. Trappings of sophisticated wealth.

The men stood, watched the president enter and take his place.

"Please." Cedric Mwanyisa motioned for them to sit. "I am deeply saddened to report that the Honorable Banda left his post as Director of Prison Corrections and Security. Not only has he failed me, and the people of our country, but he has also disappeared. Of course, I am not able to leave this position vacant considering the destabilizing factors we now face from outside forces."

The men around the table alternately experienced chilling fear and safety, somehow gratified by the fact that the wrath of their leader turned on someone else. The giddy relief of winning a game of Russian roulette.

"I have decided to replace this position with one who can bring thorough and consistent management to the area of security."

He turned and motioned to a soldier who opened the mahogany doors. A man entered and studied the other advisors gathered around the table like a man sizing up opponents. A few shifted uncomfortably in their seats. A new player on the field.

"Gentlemen, I am pleased to introduce Mr. Enoch Mpundu, our new Director of Prison Corrections and Security."

The advisors clapped politely. The new addition moved toward an open seat. A moon shaped scar hung over his ebony face.

Mpundu sat and Mwanyisa continued, "Mpundu has been tasked with finding the escaped prisoner, Gideon Chipinduka, in order to bring him to justice."

#

The faded, olive canvass on the truck fluttered in a hot breeze. The military vehicle came to a stop just outside the Harare city limits. Most people avoided the midday heat. Foot traffic was light. The driver and a passenger exited and walked to the rear of the truck. They untied a rope, slid a body from the back, dumping it on the road.

A cloud of diesel fumes swirled as they drove off.

Flies gathered, drawn to the sticky, iron smell of blood and sweat and fear. The man's polyester suit melted across several sections of his back and stomach where acid had burned into flesh. His bare feet showed similar burns and in some places, flies crawled across bare bones. Wet pants clung to his legs with a mix of urine, blood and feces.

The mass of flies lifted as the man took a shuddering breath—a drowning man reaching up. Briefly, the air was filled with the angry buzzing of flies.

Then the corpse exhaled, Banda died, and the flies grew quiet once more.

Chapter 27
Siavonga, Zambia

Colette lay by a pool overlooking Lake Kariba. Sean Wolfe had taken a taxi into Zimbabwe to arrange a houseboat from the marina there. A few boats were available on the Zambian side, but most still ran out of Zimbabwe, provided passengers could pay in US dollars and find their own fuel.

Ciro Michi told her this job was going to be different. For some reason, Michi quadrupled her usual take. He had not yet asked her to kill—though this remained a strong possibility.

According to Ciro Michi, she was here to provide dive assistance in an operation, though she knew little more. It was nice to have some time off from her regular work. Because Wolfe might not be around for the long term, there was no reason to put him on the hook, and this immediately changed the tone of where a relationship might go.

He was good looking enough, and seemed kind, though somewhat aloof. But then, she thought, what was the good of being attached to a man who just might end up dead.

What bothered Colette was Sean's apparent ambivalence about her beauty. It scared her. She didn't like to be out of control. And when she was not in control of a man in her life, she feared him.

Strange, she thought, for a woman who makes her living studying and manipulating men, for her not to have any idea how to interact with one when he wasn't a financial target. It was probably better that way, she reasoned. It would be quite difficult to continue her line of work if she actually fell in love.

She wondered what might happen if she practiced on Sean. Not falling in love, per se, just letting a man get close naturally. No con. No agendas.

Not gonna happen, she thought.

Colette rolled over and studied the blue water. She let the idea go and turned her mind, instead, to the job at hand. While she was not certain why she was needed for a diving operation in the center of Africa, she knew it was certainly illegal and probably dangerous. Furthermore, Michi must have used her because he didn't want to be connected directly. A kind of warning.

Ciro Michi always paid on time and seemed to appreciate her work as a professional. Not that she trusted the man. Since her first meeting, she found out that he mercilessly exploited the women in his brothels, turning them out on the streets after they were no longer pretty enough even under low lights to be workable whores. Most came out addicted to whatever drug was used to enslave them in the first place. They rarely lasted long on the outside.

Colette would have to find out more about what Michi was up to here. Knowing Ciro Michi made one always feel the need for some added insurance. Leverage.

Colette got up from her towel and walked to the bar. "Could I have a bottled water, please?"

The man nodded and handed her the drink.

"I'd like chicken and chips for supper. You can bring it to my room."

"Yes, madam. At what time?"

"1900 hours would be lovely," she said.

Colette thanked him, took her water and walked back to the room.

Chapter 28
Harare, Zimbabwe

Enoch Mpundu held the chicken under one arm and taped the grenade to its leg, careful to keep the trigger free. Flip-Flop stood watching some distance away, handcuffed to a rusting fence post. The bird clucked uncomfortably on the bare earth. Mpundu attached a string through the eye of the pin and played out the line until he stood a good distance away from the chicken and near his prisoner. He pulled and the chicken's leg jerked, the string wrenched the pin from the device. Mpundu smiled and counted backward from five. Before he got to one, the chicken exploded in a flash of fire and smoke and burning feathers. Flip-Flop startled violently, his eyes wide with fear and disgust.

Mpundu laughed at Flip-Flop's reaction. The chicken's head landed next to them. Mpundu picked up the head and smelled it.

"Don't forget what you have seen." He stuffed the severed head into the breast pocket of Flip-Flop's coveralls and buttoned the flap.

He led Flip-Flop past an interrogation room they visited earlier where Mpundu asked Flip-Flop vague questions about his family and made him sign his name in a ledger book. The pen hadn't worked and Mpundu merely shrugged.

Off the record.

Beyond the interrogation room stood a block shed, smaller than a chimbuzi, walls set by a poorly qualified mason. Enoch opened its iron door, shoved Flip-Flop inside and placed another grenade in his prisoner's hand.

"U noda ku kotsira?" Do you want to sleep? Enoch asked.

Flip-Flop didn't respond. Mpundu pulled the grenade pin. The door closed. A deadbolt slipped into place.

The cell wasn't much larger than a refrigerator box. Aside from two horizontal ventilation slats in the door, there was no light. Flip-Flop stared dumbly at the grenade in his hand. The green plastic bomb was clammy and slippery with sweat.

Knuckles whitened around the trigger, desperately clinging to life. Within minutes his hand cramped and the muscles in his forearm began to twitch. He considered switching the demon to the other hand, but abandoned the idea for fear that he might accidentally release the trigger. Flip-Flop set up a rotation, squeezing his hand between his knees and then under his armpit in an effort to keep the hand closed.

The setting sun left him in timeless darkness. Flip-Flop could hear nothing but his own shallow breathing and the susurration of blood in his ears.

Once he caught himself drifting off, so he banged his forehead against the cinder block until he was wide awake with pain and blinking out the blood dripping into his eyes.

Sometime in the middle of the night he had to relieve himself. Unable to undo the buttons of his coveralls, urine ran down his leg. The smell of the chicken head, and urine and sweat permeated the cell.

Too slowly the hours ticked by.

Flip-Flop started singing to stay awake. The sound of his voice filled up the empty space of time, barely keeping him from falling into a claustrophobic panic. He had no idea how long he could hold the grenade before he died.

#

Enoch Mpundu stared at the exhausted man before him. "What is your name?" he demanded.

The interrogation room was a large windowless cell. More cinder block and concrete. A drain in the floor had been installed to facilitate cleanup.

The prisoner said nothing, but stared instead at his broken shoe. Mpundu leaned forward so that his lips brushed against the man's ears. "Who was with you that day?"

Nothing. Mpundu sighed and left the room.

When Mpundu returned, Flip-Flop's toes curled around the edges of his shoes, pushing up the broken tang. The snake in Mpundu's hands tasted the room's stale air, noticed the man's fear. The angular head swayed back and forth sensing the prisoner's heat.

Mpundu held the snake so Flip-Flop would notice its bulk. Rectangular markings ran the length of richly patterned skin. Thick coils draped around Mpundu's black forearms.

"I have gone to some trouble to acquire this specimen. Perhaps you have heard of the bitis gabonica. The Gaboon Viper. It has been a pet of mine since it was a mere fingerling. The Gaboon Viper has some of the longest fangs of any snake." Mpundu smiled. "She will make you bleed out of every opening in your body, then you will die."

He walked close to the man and asked again. "What is your name?" The snake, as if on cue, stretched toward the man and flicked out its forked tongue.

"Flip-Flop. My name is Flip-Flop." Words tumbled out. No hesitation.

"What kind of name is this?" Enoch asked.

"I am also called Phillip."

"And who was with you the night you raided the prison?"

Flip-Flop tried to avoid the black eyes of the snake and its master.

Enoch stooped down, letting the snake's head fall within inches of the man's nose. Instantly Flip-Flop stiffened.

"Perhaps you did not hear my question?"

"I was drunk. I do not remember who was there." Flip-Flop tried to sound convincing, but the snake made this difficult.

Enoch laughed. "It would be much easier for you if you just told me. After we are finished I will interrogate the woman who was also there. I am sure she will tell me if you are lying.

Enoch put the snake on the ground and it began to slide toward the man whose coveralls smelled like mice. The belly scales made a soft scraping noise across the concrete.

In desperation, Flip-Flop lunged away from the snake, falling with the chair to which he was shackled. Flip-Flop lay awkwardly on the floor, tangled with the chair. The snake startled, coiled to strike.

Flip-Flop's eyes grew wide with terror. "Okay. Okay. Okay." He sputtered, flopping again in his chair, hoping to discourage the snake. "I will tell you. Only take the snake."

"I will remove the snake when you tell me who was with you."

"One man, his name was Darius. Then there was also Chuma."

"What Chuma? There are many Chuma's in town." Enoch touched the snake's tail with his shining boot, encouraging it onward.

"Davison Chuma." Flip-Flop almost shouted the name.

"And what does this man do when he is not trying to destroy our government?" Enoch asked.

"I do not know." Sweat formed about his head, standing beads that did not drip or run, but clung to his head like dew on a spider's web.

"You do not know?" The snake had moved closer to the man's trembling leg.

"Yes. I do not know."

"Who else? Tell me quickly the snake is hungry".

"There was also Danny," Flip-Flop said.

"Who is this Danny? Where is he from?"

"I do not know him. He is a white man. He was called Danny Smith."

Enoch Mpundu raised his eyebrows. This was new.

"You're lying. There are no reports of a white man there that night."

The snake moved toward a gap in the man's coveralls, drawn onward by the smell of mice that scrambled over it while the man slept in his one-room house outside of town.

"Yes. He stood in the Kiosk with the gun. I am not lying. Please sir, take the snake." Trembling overwhelmed him.

Enoch turned away from the man, leaving the snake to go where it willed. The news of a white man's involvement surprised him. It also meant the escape of Gideon Chipinduka had white support. The disgruntled white population in exile still had significant financial strength and might be able to support the escaped convict.

Flip-Flop gasped as he felt the snake's head pushing through the front opening of his coveralls, its tongue flecking against the bare skin of his trembling stomach.

Flip-Flop lost control and screamed. The snake lashed out and plunged its fangs into the man's side.

The interrogation was over.

Chapter 29
Presidential Palace
Harare, Zimbabwe

"The woman said nothing about a white man?" Mwanyisa asked. He would have preferred to conduct the interrogation himself, but he had to visit a liaison from Iran.

Enoch Mpundu absently picked dried blood from underneath his fingernails. "She said nothing of this."

"It is probable she did not see the white man. He was hiding in the Kiosk out in the street. Perhaps she did not know of him." He paused to look at the president. "Either way, I am sure she was not lying."

"That is just like a white man," Mwanyisa said, "hiding behind walls. Letting the black men run through bullets alone. Anyway, you will have to tell me about the interrogation some time."

"No," Mpundu replied boldly.

The president shot him a dangerous look.

"Why should I tell you when I have the video?" He pulled a jump drive from his pocket and handed it to the old man. "I thought you might like to see my work. Unfortunately, it did not last long. She also proved to be afraid of snakes."

A smile crossed the president's face.

Mpundu continued. "According to security reports, Mr. Smith left the country for Zambia. It should be easy enough to find him there. A white stone in a black wall is not hard to locate. But the fact that

111

he was in league with Davison Chuma and your rival, Gideon Chipinduka, makes him still quite dangerous."

Mwanyisa stared into the face of his advisor. "I have no rivals. These are only inconveniences that stand in the way of the future of my country. What about Chipinduka and Chuma?" Mwanyisa asked. "Where have they gone?"

Mpundu reached into a thin case and pulled out a sheet of paper. An embassy informant told me they have gone into hiding somewhere in Europe. Their exact location is unknown."

"Europe is a big place. Mr. Daniel Smith will know their whereabouts. We find Mr. Smith; we can find the others—though they are nothing more than fleas on my back."

Mwanyisa stared out the window. "I go to Zambia in a few days for the SADC convention. I will have significant exposure throughout the conference. The inconvenience of Mr. Smith must be taken care of before I arrive. I trust you are capable of dealing with this new threat to national security?"

Enoch smiled. "It will be my pleasure."

Chapter 30
Mazabuka, Zambia

Mazabuka began as one of the Crown's largest sugar holdings. It remained in possession of the Crown Prince until the late 1990's when he needed cash and was forced to sell off assets in the former colony. While most commercial farms were in the hands of Zambia's white farmers, Mazabuka was home to a large population of Tonga. Many Tonga found seasonal wage labor on the cane farms and their employers did their best to supplement wages with decent health care. Though not much could be done for people living with HIV/AIDS, malaria was still the number one killer and it could be treated fairly easily.

Kathy Hall made herself useful in the Mazabuka farming community. Though Kathy had no medical training, she knew enough to assist in the clinic run by the farmer's co-operative. Though a government clinic nearby offered highly subsidized services, it chronically ran short on medicines and frequently lacked supplies like syringes and needles required for administering basic treatment.

Kathy stood at the pharmacists table and counted out a prescription for a particularly bad case of malaria. The nurse, who graduated from the Lusaka School of Nursing, had at first been shy about directing a white assistant. Kathy soon had her laughing, and they got along fine.

For Kathy, long days in the clinic kept her from thinking of home, or her husband's involvement in what was turning out to be a small-scale revolution. She wasn't surprised when he told her. It was not the first time he had gone off to war, but Kathy was astute enough to notice Sheila withdrawing into herself.

Like Sheila, Kathy would have been content to settle into Zambia and try to forget the past. Somehow, that seemed much safer than what Stuart and the others had planned, but she knew her husband well enough to see when he had his mind set on a course of action.

They numbly made the necessary contingency plans, working out all the details against the possibility of his death. It seemed surreal enough for her to remain somewhat detached, but she knew an idle mind would drive her mad.

Kathy folded the paper into an envelope. She tipped the measuring plate and the white pills slid off into the packet. "There you go, Mary. I think this is the last one." She looked through the window at a line forming outside the dispensary.

"Do you have anything else for me to do, boss?" she asked.

"Maybe you should go and check on the twins."

Mary knew her assistant loved the smallest patients the best and helped invent excuses for Kathy to visit the ICU. The 'Intensive Care Unit' offered seven beds. Occasionally, the clinic would see complicated lacerations related to unfortunate accidents with farm machinery or knife wounds, but unless it required straightforward surgery, these usually transferred to a hospital. Most of the beds served complicated maternity cases. Recently, a mother carried in by family members on a litter, successfully delivered twin girls. Afterward, the mother hemorrhaged badly and had to be taken to the Catholic hospital in Choma, just an hour away. The twins stayed behind at the clinic.

The ICU smelled of Africa and disinfectant. There were seven beds in total with as many infant cots in between.

"Mwabuka buti?" Kathy greeted a young mother in the first bed who silently encouraged her infant to nurse.

"Kabotu." The woman replied, but her eyes were anxious. The newborn seemed unimpressed by the proffered nipple and instead lay sleeping with one fist curled up against the side of a wrinkled face.

Kathy helped the girl unwrap her baby to wake it up. Gently she worked the baby's legs until the miniature fist began to tremble slightly and a squeak rose from pouting lips. Kathy turned the child toward her mother's breast and watched it begin to nurse.

Two bundles shared the same cot toward the end of the ward. Their heads rested at opposite sides, barely filling the cot.

"They have just eaten." A girl sat in a wooden chair near the twins. Grace, a nervous ten year old, had been left behind to look after the twins in the absence of her mother. Grace's English was good and she smiled when Kathy checked in on them. Kathy paid for the formula herself and showed Grace how to prepare it.

A family member usually served as nurse aid in the clinic and provided meals for the patient. Kathy picked up one of the little bundles and sat down on the empty bed. She rocked gently and sang a Shona song she remembered from her childhood Sunday-School class.

Chapter 31
Mazabuka, Zambia

Daniel opened the CD case and inserted the half-size disk into his laptop. He sat on a stool in front of a table made from a few boxes.

Green mosquito coils smoldered around him. He moved them closer in an effort to discourage the minute phlebotomists.

He punched another button on the keyboard, waited for the application to load. Somehow he had managed to get up without waking Sheila. While she slept, she wrapped herself around him, but during the day she would barely make eye contact. She planned to head to Lusaka on Saturday and fly to London the following day.

The screen blinked to life and Daniel hit 'play'. This was not the first time he had seen the recording. Stuart had given it to him just before they left Zimbabwe.

"I found this in your house." Stuart said when he handed Daniel the camcorder. "I noticed the light blinking when I came to fetch Sheila. It was set up on a tripod in the corner of your room." He looked thoughtfully at his son-in-law. "I'm afraid it's pretty hard to watch. I don't think Sheila knows about it."

The first time he saw it, Daniel shook with rage.

The screen blinked on. Showed a picture of his old bedroom. A man walked to the front of the camera and crouched down. A face filled the screen, silhouetted against the lighted window behind. The man adjusted the camera, orienting it to record the bedroom and through to the adjacent bathroom.

Daniel watched his wife's nightmare. He gripped the edge of the box when the man hit Sheila, sending her sprawling. Just afterwards, the man turned back to glance at the camera and Daniel paused the screen.

Selecting the face, Daniel copied the image to another program, enlarging it as much as he could without ruining the resolution. He sent the image to a borrowed printer sitting on the floor.

He stared into the man's face.

"I will find you."

Chapter 32
Lake Kariba, Zambia
Friday, March 5

Onboard diesel engines rumbled and *The Paradise* slipped away from the dock. Colette Logan stood on the stern of the houseboat and watched a few hippos, lazing in the water, drop away in a swirl of mud and white bubbles. Sean Wolfe had been friendly enough when he returned with the charter but had yet to explain her part. She still had no idea what scheme she'd fallen into, but she knew it was big. She determined again to find information to use as leverage.

She couldn't shake the feeling that she might be expendable. She wanted to trust Ciro Michi. In a way, Colette had developed a kind of paternal affection for the old man. He was, after all, the first man to show an interest in more than her body and his efforts in developing her skills felt like a fatherly blessing.

The lake resort disappeared from view as Wolfe turned out of the bay and followed the shore toward Siavonga. Here and there, a mud brick house with a corrugated roof peeked out from the brush on the bank. They passed a man paddling a dugout, his fishing net heaped over his catch. Colette smiled and waved. It didn't hurt to make sure she was noticed.

The houses began to crowd together, becoming more substantial as they drew closer to the lake town. They rounded a bend and drew into the marina. Colette noticed a red brick house built on a steep bank designed to have a commanding view. The carport, however, had flooded. She guessed the surveyor miscalculated the water level. That or the dam authorities did what they wanted. Damn authorities.

She smiled at her own joke.

Wolfe eased back the throttle and steered toward a wooden pier jutting out beside a muddy boat launch. Fishing boats returned from their shift moored in the marina and the area crowded with women tending thickly woven baskets of fresh bream. The market looked like an afterthought, and smelled of sweat and rain and fish.

A black man with a red baseball cap tied their boat to the pier and greeted them both. Wolfe followed him toward a pickup truck and trailer.

Colette dallied in the market, listening to the sounds of women laughing and calling her to see their baskets of fish. The Tonga women dressed in bright, traditional cottons. Dead fish, packed in ice, lay staring at her from the baskets, glassy eyed and unblinking.

"You want to buy fish?" A woman held up a bream for Colette to inspect.

"Yes." Colette smiled and thought, *be seen*. Make friends. Insurance, need insurance. She noticed a child tied to the woman's back with a length of cloth. "How much for the fish?"

The woman grew serious and said, "Two thousand kwacha."

"For how many?" Colette responded and the women around them laughed. Their laughter came easily. She wondered what that might be like. Colette reached out to touch the head peeking out from patterned cloth. "How old is your baby?" she asked.

"Two weeks," the woman replied.

"She is beautiful." It was true. A white crocheted cap engulfed the tiny head. "The baby must be hot." Colette herself could feel the heat and the humid smell of fresh fish pressing in on her.

"No. He is happy."

"I'm sorry. It is not a girl?"

"Yes," the woman replied. Colette wasn't sure where that left the child's gender.

She glanced around to find Wolfe and Red Cap trying to back the trailer toward the end of the pier. They appeared to be having some difficulty. Good, she thought, more time. "Do you have other children?" Colette asked.

"Yes," the woman replied with a single proud nod.

"How many?" The others gathered to join the conversation. One of them chattered something to the group and a ripple of laughter followed. Colette imagined she was the joke, but it didn't feel unfriendly.

The same woman addressed the mother with a volley of words Colette didn't understand.

"Seven," came the reply.

"Seven? How can you have seven children? You are so young."

Colette glanced back again. The men unloaded something onto the pier. Time to go.

"Then I will take seven fish," Colette said. More laughter.

The vendor rummaged through her basket, making a show of finding the best fish for her new friend. These she carefully placed in a thin plastic bag with a handful of ice. Colette wondered where they found ice in a town like this. Certainly a few houses belonged to wealthy people, but most of the town looked like it had fallen out of the sky and stayed splayed out wherever it landed.

She pulled three blue kwacha notes from her pocket. The woman sucked in her breath in surprise at the amount of cash. While a single ten-pin note was worth only two dollars, the overpayment would make her week.

After waving to the baby, Colette walked back toward *The Paradise*. Wolfe and Red Cap hefted a generator and what looked like a compressor onto the covered area at the stern. Wolfe's shoulders squared in a non-sculpted sort of way. Colette noticed. A man made strong by real work, not in a gym. Sweat streaked their faces and made dark wet patches on their chests. Several wooden crates were still on the pick-up. She didn't try to carry anything. Instead, she stood watching, trying to solve the puzzle of this job.

What could they possibly be up to in a place like this? There was nothing here anyone would want, except water.

#

Wolfe hired on one man to serve as chef, captain and housekeeper. The hire was precautionary. Few houseboats left without a crew, and Wolfe didn't want to raise questions. They would be able to keep him out of the way at the right time. The young fellow had been a cook for one of the better hotels on the Zimbabwe side until the drop in tourist activity precipitated his unemployment. With the cash Wolfe had given him, he'd managed to procure from

Siavonga the ingredients they needed to remain well supplied on their trip. Wolfe helped him load the booze and groceries.

The first evening they anchored just off Fathergill Island and ate by candle light while listening to the hippo's guttural calls. Storms danced above the water in the distance and the screens on the boat kept mosquitoes to a minimum. In other circumstances, it might have been romantic.

"You should have stayed on the boat at Siavonga," Wolfe said. Candlelight played across her face, making her look darker than he remembered.

"Why should I?" she asked.

"Because we aren't here on holiday. Besides, the fewer people who see you on the boat, the better."

"So when you drop me off the boat no one will bother about me?" Her tone was soft, even friendly, but Wolfe realized she wasn't kidding.

He put down his fork and leaned back in his chair. "I don't know what our mutual contact told you about your work here." He paused to wipe his mouth on the serviette. "Frankly, I was a little surprised."

"Surprised? How is that?" she asked.

"That he sent a woman."

"Does this arrangement make you uncomfortable?" Though she had determined not to work this man, she left a hint of suggestion in her voice.

He studied her a moment longer. "No. It does not. However, our mutual contact has a reputation."

"What kind of reputation?" Colette asked with feigned ignorance.

"I cannot believe that you are unaware of his business dealings, but I will humor you."

Having finished his supper, Sean pushed back his chair and crossed his legs. "Ciro Michi has a reputation for always getting what he wants. Always. As long as I have been alive, there has never been an exception to that. Not even once. Though I fully expect to make him a lot of money on this deal, I am not yet officially a member of his "family", and this makes him nervous, I think.

"Ciro Michi has built his empire on the backs of others, and he is the kind of man who is cautious. In my opinion, the fact that he sent a beautiful woman to serve as my assistant is not merely a matter of chance. Because you are beautiful, I expect it is for some special reason that you were selected. Perhaps it is to keep an eye on me. Perhaps he has asked you to seduce me. Either way, the fact that you have been chosen means two things."

She raised her eyebrows in question, so he continued.

"First of all it means that you are exactly the person he wanted for this job, and secondly, it means that you, also, are in an equal amount of danger. The bottom line is I have no reason to trust you. And you should know, neither of us have any reason to trust Ciro Michi."

While Colette had attempted to keep her best poker face, Wolfe's words sent a chill through her body. She knew he was right.

"I know Michi, though likely not as well as you. I am not from Italy," she responded.

This was true, Wolfe had already decided. Her accent sounded like a cross between an English woman and something else. It was the something else that confused him.

"However," Colette continued, "while Michi is paying me for my work, I am, like you, self-employed." She paused to decide how much to tell him and swirled the last of the beer in her glass. "I think you are correct, on both fronts. This man always gets what he wants. Unfortunately, neither you nor I know what he has planned for our futures."

"Yet. Assuming you speak the truth," Wolfe added. "At some point, Michi may let you or I know. When that happens, we may both find ourselves out of favor with the other. Though I would like to believe we are both on the same team, I understand Michi may decide to play us against each other." He paused to sip his drink. "Until the job is over, you must forgive me if I do not share your bed."

For one of the few times in her life, Colette blushed with shame. Shame not from his comment, but because it cut dangerously close to the truth. The reality that she could not manipulate Wolfe frightened her. She stood, pushed in her chair, and set down her glass before slapping him hard across his face.

Chapter 33
Near Mazabuka, Zambia
Friday, March 5

Kathy and Grace each carried one of the babies for the long walk to their village. Their mother had not completely recovered in Choma, but limited space in the Mazabuka clinic precluded a longer stay for the twins.

For almost an hour they had followed the narrow twisting footpaths beside fields and now seemed lost in the bush. Kathy hoped Grace would be willing to show her the way back.

When Grace had said her village was 'not far', Kathy had asked Mary, her 'boss', for more specific details.

"Mary, do you know where Grace and the twins live? I'd like to go along with her to help carry the twins."

"I have heard of the village, but I've never been there," Mary replied.

"Grace said it isn't far. What does that mean?"

Mary laughed. "'Not far' means you can walk there in only half a day."

Kathy paused on the trail and put down her basket and switched the baby to the other arm. What was I thinking, she asked herself. There is no way I could have driven them home anyway, she thought, looking at the footpath through the trees. At least it isn't raining. Grace took the basket for her, and they started off again. The girl seemed unfazed by the journey and the hot sun put the twins to sleep.

They stopped several more times before reaching the village, once to feed the babies and again because Kathy asked for it. When they walked into the village clearing, Kathy wasn't sure she could make the return journey on the same day.

The family village consisted of a few huts and a round, open-sided thatched shelter. A brown goat, picketed to a rough post, stretched its neck to nibble at weeds beyond its reach. Several women greeted them, inviting Kathy into the shade and offering her a stool. She gratefully accepted and watched as they chattered around the twins and carried them over to see their father.

The man sat in the shade of his own hut, smoking a carved pipe. He glanced briefly at his new children and walked to the thatched shelter where Kathy sat waiting.

"Mwabuka buti?" How are you? Kathy asked. Her Tonga didn't extend beyond greetings.

"Kabotu," he replied.

The man looked three times older than his wife. Another woman brought him a stool, and he sat opposite Kathy in the enclosure, leaning up against the rough-hewn poles. He smelled strongly of smoke and sweat and age. His yellowed eyes held a kind of unnatural intensity that made Kathy uncomfortable.

It dawned on her that the other women in the village were also his wives.

One of these brought her an enamel cup filled with local beer. She thanked the woman who dipped a deferential curtsy in return.

Kathy took a sip and chewed the maize. It bubbled a little in her mouth but, she was too thirsty and the drink was hearty and probably strong. Better not to think about how it was made.

The old man spoke about his fields and children and the rains. They stumbled along in awkward English. She appreciated his attempts. Kathy tried to explain his youngest wife's medical condition. His face remained unmoved and detached as he listened. Kathy didn't bother to go through formula directions. Grace would have to remember her lessons.

The man leaned forward and swept a place smooth in the dirt before him. He withdrew an assortment of bones from the skin bag at his side.

"Bring me beer." One of the three women who sat on the mat next to Kathy left to get the drink.

She returned with a gourd filled with the fermented beer. He motioned with his head to a post planted off to the side. The woman took the gourd and poured the libation onto the ground at its base. It looked like a branch of some tree about the size and shape of a fence post that had been planted. It had sprouted a single shoot and a few leaves. Proof of the ancestors' power.

The man hocked and spat into the dirt, chanting incoherent incantations. A chill settled across Kathy's shoulders. Witch doctors still held considerable power but she herself had never visited one. Her own father had, on occasion, consulted the local medicine man on matters of rain and rinderpest but never told her mother, who believed medicine men were of the devil.

He squatted on the ground by his earthy tablet, eyes closed and body rocking.

He moved closer and stirred the air around Kathy's face with a cow-tail fly swish mounted on an ornamented handle.

Kathy felt the heady rush of beer and a lifting sensation as she listened to the hiss of the tail near her ears. Her hands and arms began to tingle and she watched dispassionately as darkness began to close around her vision, growing ever narrower until there was only blackness and the hiss of the tail.

Kathy knew she could not move, even if she wanted to. The hiss and the cool darkness and the beer made her desperate for sleep. She would have been happy to slump to the ground right there on the swept dirt floor. Yet she remained fastened to her stool, listening and seeing only darkness until a new sound began in the distance. African drums in a dissynchronous rhythm played chase with the eerie sound of an odd flute. The notes and the beat tangled with each other for a moment, then lifted, each going its own way. Again they returned, closer now, working into her mind, as if they followed familiar hallways deeper into an old house. The flute grew stronger. Its melancholy sound now like the wailing women at a funeral, now the shrill call of a bird. The drum beat throbbed in her ears. It mingled with the pulse of her own heart reaching to her finger tips and toes.

Then the sound began to slow her heart and the notes grew longer, sadder.

Words formed among the music. The voices of women and children. They spoke in Shona, the language of her childhood nanny. The voices pleaded, "Hurry, hurry." All the same. "Help us, help us. The waters are coming." The drum and music carried the cry along like so many leaves upon water. The call repeated itself in Bantu languages she did not recognize.

All pleaded for help. All carried the fear of water. Faces resolved from darkness. Voices mixed with music, stirred together, heaped up on each other for a time, cried out singly or in groups. At one point Kathy heard the sound of Portuguese. Separate and distinct from the others, yet still pleading. But the faces, the faces she saw were all the same. Gripped in panic, lined with fear and terror. Drowning mouths open in one last desperate cry for rescue.

The sound of water ran under the drum and flute and screaming, growing louder, ever louder, taking up more and more space in her mind until she too was screaming for it to stop, so she might help the people. One woman lifted her child above gathering black water, tried to keep it above the death surrounding her, begged Kathy to take it. But the water came on. Kathy tried to cover her ears, but remembered she could not move. She could only watch waters rise, listen to the screaming, unable to reach out for the child's hand extended now alone above unfeeling water. One single tiny hand stretched out of the vast expanse of gathering water, one last reaching for life.

The noise and music stopped, but the empty silence of death and water seemed to go on forever.

Kathy awakened to the sound of sobbing. A bare necked chicken strutted across the swept earth and the medicine man dozed in the shade of his own hut where she had first noticed him. The women were gone, probably to the fields. Kathy felt tears on her arms and sat up to wipe her eyes, realized the sobbing was her own.

After a few minutes, Grace walked around the corner of a hut and came toward her.

"I will escort you home," Grace said.

"Thank you." Kathy wondered if she could stand. Shaken, she got to her feet and stooped under the thatched eve into the sunshine. The ground was wet and water dripped from trees overhead. It had rained.

Kathy glanced back at the old man. "Grace, when did your father learn to speak Shona?"

Grace looked confused. Shook her head. "My father speaks only Tonga and Lala."

Gwembe was the only language in Zimbabwe that held similarities to Tonga, it being the same language in the days before the construction of the Kariba Dam. Since then, the lake interfered with the northern and southern tribesmen and their language grew more disparate.

Grace saw the drawings her father had made by Kathy's stool and added, "But the spirits, they can speak Shona."

Chapter 34
Mazabuka, Zambia
Saturday, March 6

Sheila stared at the mosquito net and the plastic soda crates that served as makeshift night stands and tried to decide what she should take. In truth, there was nothing else. Almost everything had been left behind in Zimbabwe. Her house. Her dogs. Her marriage.

Daniel said nothing when she threatened to leave. Nothing. Only numb silence. She wanted him to fight for her. Beg her to stay.

She would head up to Lusaka, stay overnight at a guest house and take the first flight out on Sunday. Sheila closed her suitcase and carried it to the living room. Its borrowed furniture looked lost.

Daniel appeared in the open doorway, silhouetted against the sky beyond.

"Are you going to drive me to the airport, or will I have to get a cab?" The matter of fact words belied the way she felt.

He just stood there and stared. "It wasn't supposed to end like this," he said.

"You weren't supposed to run off to war." She fought to keep the tremor out of her voice.

"I'll drive you." He didn't move.

"I'm ready to go," she said. Already her mind swirled with fear and stress and fatigue.

"I understand if you must go," Daniel said, "but before you leave there is something I have to show you."

He walked to his makeshift desk and picked up a manila file. "Why don't we sit down for a minute?"

He pulled up a chair and handed her the file. She hesitated, then opened it. On the top was the enlarged portrait Daniel had made. Sheila exploded, shoved the file off her lap, sending pictures all over the floor. "Where did you get those?"

"His name is Enoch Mpundu. According to our information, he has just been appointed the director of Prison Corrections and Security for Mwanyisa."

"What made you think I'd want to see this?"

"Sheila, since all this began you haven't been the same. You are afraid. Even here. I hear you talking in your sleep, calling for the dogs. I see you walking around the place, like you've lost something and can't find it."

"So you think showing me a photo of that monster is going to help?"

"I got this from your dad." He motioned to the pictures on the floor. "That man set up our camera to record his 'meeting' with you. I guess he wanted to be sure his message came through."

Sheila looked like a frightened animal. "Please don't ask me to watch that." Her voice tiny and childlike.

"Don't worry. You don't have to see it," he stopped and picked up the pictures, putting them back in the file, "but I'm keeping these."

Sheila stood and reached for her suitcase. "I have to get out of here. I'll ask mother to drive me."

Daniel grabbed her arm. "I am going to kill him, too, Sheila. I want you to feel safe again. Likely he will be traveling with the president. I won't rest until he is dead. Then I will come and get you."

"Come with me now." Tears ran down her face.

"I want to come. But if I come now I will always be haunted by knowing I left something behind. Something I was supposed to do."

"So you are going to abandon me for Africa?" Her voice was small again.

"Luv, if you want me to be loyal, then I have to be loyal to everything important in my life. If I don't finish this thing, then it changes the man I am—the man you married."

Sheila knuckled tears from her eyes, came and stood right in front of him—close enough to kiss. "You're a fool," she whispered.

Chapter 35
The Paradise
Lake Kariba, Zambia
Saturday, March 6

Colette stood barefoot by the railing, sipping coffee when Sean Wolfe came out.

Instead of turning, she pointed to the bank where an elephant and her calf had come for a morning drink.

He joined her and leaned on the rail to watch. The great beasts seemed completely at ease with their visitors and continued the contented, guttural rumbling of elephant talk.

"I wonder what they are saying," Colette mused, the incident from the previous night temporarily set aside. "Isn't it beautiful?"

Wolfe looked at her. "Yes."

Their cabin boy brought Wolfe steaming black coffee and for a time, they did not speak, but watched the creatures drink the glassy water and move off slowly into the bush.

"I must apologize for my comment last night," Wolfe said, absently touching his face. "I shouldn't let my opinion of our employer color those he hires."

She turned to see if he was sincere then looked at the retreating elephants. "How is your face?"

He smiled wryly. "I will say I have never been slapped by a more beautiful woman. Shall we get started?"

"No," Colette replied. "First, I want details. Then I will decide if I want to continue."

"Fair enough," Wolfe shrugged. He reached for a pair of binoculars. "The Kariba Dam is over there." He motioned vaguely to the northeast where the low line of hills surrounding them came together on the horizon. "This dam was built over fifty years ago. Owners of several mining interests in the north formed a consortium with other investors. These investors saw the Zambezi River as a cash cow waiting to be harnessed for cheap electricity. Electricity needed to run mines in what was then Northern and Southern Rhodesia. Cesar Fournier, the project's civil engineer, pioneered the design for double curvature arch dams like Kariba. But his work contained some errors."

"What kind of errors," Colette asked.

"His calculations were impeccable, but according to Esposito—the engineer for whom we're working—Fournier failed to take into consideration the possibility of seismic activity."

"Is there a fault line here?" Colette asked.

"Yes and no," Wolfe explained. "The Zambezi River follows the western edge of an ancient fault line responsible for forming the Great Rift Valley. Though it has not seen dramatic activity for quite some time, it remains, technically, active. There is still, in fact, volcanic activity along the fault in the north.

"Fournier failed to foresee a phenomena that has not until recently been identified. Kariba remains one of the largest man-made lakes on the planet. It holds an estimated 186 billion cubic meters of water. The combined weight has a similar effect to standing on the edge of a coffee table."

"It begins to tip." Colette listened with fascinated horror.

"Yes. The plates tip. Tectonic activity. Since the late fifties, when the dam began to fill, over twenty earthquakes have been recorded exceeding five on the Richter scale. The southern end of the Rift Valley fault has grown increasingly unstable. When the area faces unprecedented seasonal rainfalls, as they are now, the possibility of a major earthquake increases."

"And you are here because you care deeply about the welfare of those below the dam," Colette said. "I didn't know Michi had friends like that."

"I never said he was my friend," Wolfe replied. "Our job here is to generate a few harmless cracks in the dam wall so international aid organizations in conjunction with the Zambian and Zimbabwean governments will be convinced to finance a repair."

"So you and Ciro Michi have gone into humanitarian work?"

Wolfe smiled, "Esposito has good reason to believe the firm he works for will be awarded the contract for this repair. It is, as you can imagine, expensive work." He shrugged as if the rest were obvious. He said exactly what he had been told to say and watched to see if she believed him. Satisfied, he continued. "What we need to do is, of course, quite dangerous."

"Dangerous how?" Colette asked.

"Dangerous because Michi is involved, paying to move materials quickly through international borders. He's provided someone who can complete the underwater component without needing to go to confession." He feigned a deferential bow and crossed himself irreverently. "It is also dangerous because you will be working at night in crocodile infested waters. And if we are discovered, we will be shot."

Colette frowned. "That could be painful." She held the binoculars to her eyes and studied the hills. "Well then," she concluded, "we'll just have to make sure we don't get caught."

"Good. Today we prepare our equipment. I've already asked the chef to take us toward the mouth of the N'Gatchi-Gatchi River. Tomorrow night we begin our work on the wall. Let's hope the crocodiles aren't hungry."

"What about him?" Colette nodded toward the galley.

"He will sleep well tonight," Wolfe replied.

#

Colette wondered that Arturo Esposito's plan was darker than Wolfe had suggested. In spite of customs risks, Colette had smuggled in her 38 revolver. The Rossi by Taurus carried five rounds and was compact enough to be inconspicuous under casual dress. A bullet was terribly messy, and harder to clean up than most people imagined. Still, Michi had hinted this business might get nasty, and so she hadn't come naked.

Knowing what she knew of man's greed, she doubted Esposito's firm—in league with Ciro Michi—would be content with merely repairing a few cracks if they could land a more lucrative project.

But she guarded her mind against considering the broader implications. What she already knew afforded some leverage and could be translated into significant wealth, if she was careful. Balanced. This could get complicated. She would need proof.

Chapter 36
Lusaka, Zambia
Saturday, March 6

The Southern African Development Community or SADC is a regional association of the sovereign states of Southern Africa, including a few nearby—and not so nearby—islands. Created to resemble the European Union of Southern Africa it grew to become both broader in scope and less effective in its aim to improve regional cooperation and facilitate free trade.

Heads of state gathered every two years for the SADC convention where they ostensibly dealt with inter-trade agreements, power sharing and water rights. In truth, lesser men handled these matters and were not invited. The convention presented an occasion for fanfare, handshaking and political peacocking.

This year Zambia played host for the convention and preparations at the venue were almost complete. The public events, rallies and parades were to be held at the Lusaka show grounds, while the eating and more intimate gatherings would be hosted by the Protea Hotel just north of town. The Protea Hotel Corporation operates out of South Africa and caters to well moneyed clients, including international dignitaries, wealthy tourists, and Peace Corps volunteers on holiday. What is more, the owners of the chain held no strong political views, save those that favored the development of their franchise in Africa with as little red tape as possible.

The franchise determined to promote itself by providing a stunning experience for guests. Preparations were made, chefs hired, wild game procured to augment what already roamed their grounds, and the bars stocked with the best Southern African wines.

Operating on a well-treed and manicured property, the hotel itself consisted of an elegant thatched conference room, open to the outside with a low stone wall around its perimeter. The stand-alone suites mirrored the thick rounded thatch of the dinning and convention hall and offered mosquito nets romantically draped across carved ebony frames. Cool flagstone covered the floor and en suite baths offered luxury of a kind that was opulent and distinctly African in flavor.

Each room had been supplied with its own wet bar and furnishings tailored to appeal to the particular tastes of its occupant and guest. Training for the vetted staff and housecleaning employees had been exciting, extensive and exhausting. Now with the big event only a few weeks away, the final pieces were falling into place.

Chapter 37
Mazabuka, Zambia
Saturday, March 6

Stuart was pleased. Chuma informed him as soon as he received final confirmation that Mwanyisa would indeed be attending. The leader seldom left the country anymore. Stuart suspected it was shame, but perhaps the old buzzard had calluses on his soul. Who knew?

Mwanyisa's reputation resulted in a dwindling number of invitations from the international community beyond the SADC nations. SADC nations found it easier to befriend the monster next door than pick a fight.

That Mwanyisa planned to attend the convention despite his reputation, Stuart found quite interesting. In all likelihood, the man saw this as an opportunity to feed his ego, even if it required the strained platitudes of his peers. Stuart shook his head. Mwanyisa didn't have to carry a banner with a picture of the failed Zimbabwean dollar. Everyone knew the money had recently earned the distinction of being the fastest inflating currency in recorded history.

Stuart reached for a marker and leaned over his map. The presidential parade would travel from the fair-grounds to the north end roundabout and then onto the Great North Road. Their best opportunity would come just before Mwanyisa's vehicle left the outskirts of town. That would give ample time for Stuart's men to make a getaway amidst the more sparsely populated sprawl surrounding the townships.

He thumbed the lid off the marker and placed three dots on his map. From these three dots he drew black lines toward a single point on the Great North Road. The intersecting lines made a neat little asterisk on the map.

"Bang," Stuart whispered. "You're dead."

Chapter 38
Lusaka, Zambia
Sunday, March 7

Sheila handed the driver her fare and wheeled her suitcase into the terminal. The Lusaka International Airport connected the south central African region and reached to points as far north as Amsterdam and London

A bronze kudu dominated a corner of the broadly tiled lobby. The British Airways ticket office opened after lunch. The terminal carried the muted echoes of people disembarking from the BA flight that had just arrived. An attendant in blue appeared at the BA desk.

Sheila walked up to the counter. "Good morning, I would like to book a seat on the first available flight to London."

"Good morning. And will you be traveling alone?" The attendant moused her way to a new screen.

Sheila waited for the lump in her throat to subside. "Yes," she managed.

"You're in luck. We have space on the plane that just arrived. It will be here for a few hours for cleaning. Departure is schedule for 1400 hours. Would that be too soon for you?"

"That will be fine, thank you," Sheila replied. "One way, please."

The attendant busied herself with her computer. "We have available seating in business and first class. What would you prefer?"

"Business is fine." Sheila slid a credit card across the desk. She had hoped to walk in, get on the plane and leave her nightmare behind. Now she would be forced to wait. To think. And thinking was intolerable.

The attendant retrieved the printout and showed Sheila her seat number before folding the ticket into a blue envelope. "Have a lovely flight."

"Thank you." Sheila stuffed the ticket into her bag and tried to decide what to do while she waited. She had not bothered to contact her grandparents in England. They didn't know she was coming. Having to explain that her marriage was already in shambles felt too complicated. They had even come to Zimbabwe for the wedding hosted on the green lawns of Peacock Farm. Perhaps she could just send them an email. Her phone didn't have an international SIM card. Time enough to find an internet café in town, get a coffee and pretend her life was intact.

The taxi drivers and hustlers swarmed, determined to help with her suitcase.

She picked one of the drivers. "Please take me to the internet café at Manda Hill." She didn't care what he charged.

He stowed the suitcase; she settled herself in the passenger seat. A soldier waved them through the military checkpoint just beyond terminal parking. The man with the machine gun seemed unconcerned with the taxi.

They passed a sport utility vehicle heading toward the airport. Blue letters spelled W.H.O. across the door. Sheila happened to glance at the passing driver and her blood ran cold. How was that possible? But she had seen the unmistakable scar. The face in her nightmares. Enoch Mpundu. Sheila sank down in her seat and begged the driver to hurry.

He complied with a simple, "No problem."

She glanced behind. The SUV had stopped at the checkpoint. The taxi turned a sweeping corner and she could no longer see.

"Can I trust you?" She had little time and desperately needed an ally.

"Yes, madam," he replied.

She decided to chance it. "That man we just passed, I can't let him see me. Please drive quickly."

He looked in his rear view and replied again, "No problem." Sheila huddled low and the taxi jerked as the vehicle hurled off the tar road. Tires slued in mud. Water from a puddle hammered underneath.

"I'm supposed be at the airport in two hours, but I don't think I'll be able to get through customs without him finding me. Do you know of a place where I can hide?" she asked.

He nodded. "Yes. No problem." He swerved around a pothole.

She wondered if he really understood what she was saying. "Is he following us?"

"Yes, but they have stayed on the main road." Sheila peeked over the driver and saw blue letters on white disappear around a bend in the road, speeding back toward downtown Lusaka.

Now she was certain. He was looking for her.

"This man, he is dangerous?" her driver asked.

"Yes." Sheila paused and said. "Look, I will pay you anything you ask. Just please help me get away from him."

"No madam. I do not charge for this thing." The vehicle lurched again as they splashed through another puddle, brown water sluicing off the sides.

"Where are you taking me?" Sheila asked.

"Because you are a white woman, it is more difficult to hide." He seemed to be thinking. "I know a woman who can help you."

Sheila wanted an army, not some woman, but she let it go, hoping his broken English had accounted for the error in number and gender.

From her place low in the car, Sheila could now see broken-glass-topped walls. Trees lined the streets. Probably some kind of residential area. He made several turns and continually studied his rear view for a tail. Her driver pulled his cellphone from its place on the seat, punched in a number and held it to his ear.

"Salaam." He spoke into the phone then babbled on in a local Bantu dialect that was otherwise incomprehensible to her.

The phone snapped shut and they pulled abruptly to a stop in front of an iron gate. He honked his horn once and waited for the gatekeeper to peek out the window of the guard shack.

The gate squeaked open and her driver accelerated into the yard sending up a spray of gravel. "They have not followed us here. But I must leave quickly and find another white woman, so they can think they have followed the wrong cab when they find me." He got out of the vehicle and removed her suitcase.

She reached into her purse to remove some cash for payment and held it out toward him.

He refused the money. "Please. No problem." Then he climbed into the blue taxi, the gate squeaked closed, and he was gone.

A fountain gurgled in a shady corner under a palm tree. A manicured garden surrounded the house. The watchman disappeared in his shack. For a long minute Sheila stood beside her suitcase wondering what had happened.

Chapter 39
Lusaka, Zambia
Sunday, March 7

Standing alone in the driveway of a stranger's house, Sheila felt the stress of her world caving in on her. Her knees began to tremble, so she sat down on the suitcase. Mpundu's face and the horror of her failing marriage seemed like a nightmare that should belong to someone else.

Through her tears she saw a door open and a woman approach wearing a long burqa without the head covering. Perhaps this was why the security guard so quickly retreated. Likely the owner moved freely in her own garden.

The robe nearly touched the tops of her bare feet. "Welcome to my home. My brother called and told me that you were in danger." She noticed Sheila's face. "Please, I will help you inside." The blue burqa accentuated the beauty of her black skin.

She took one of Sheila's arms and picked up the suitcase. Together they walked to the front door and stepped into the cool shade of curtained windows and marble-tiled floors. She noted Sheila's surprise at the posh décor and shrugged. "My husband is a wealthy man. He exports gems to Iran. Please, sit here." A row of cushions rested along the wall. "My husband will also welcome you. He is a man of God and will take it as a matter of honor to see you taken care of."

Sheila had not yet said a word, but the realities of her life and the completely unexpected gesture of kindness again unleashed the flow of tears. Her body shook with sobs. When Sheila's grief spent itself, her host got up and returned with a cup of sweet coffee and a plate of dried fruit and nuts.

"My name is Annie Asgari. My brother just called and told me he found another white woman who was willing to ride in his taxi." She set the fruit plate on a low coffee table. "He has friends at the Catholic mission. The nuns know he is a good man and always call him when they need a taxi." A look of concern crossed her face. "But he was stopped and questioned."

"Then he *was* looking for me," Sheila said, almost to herself. She had allowed herself to hope Mpundu had been on some other business in the country. It was a lot to hope. Maybe Daniel was right. Maybe he had to kill the man, so she could be safe. She buried her face in her hands, too tired to cry anymore, too exhausted to think.

"Yes, the man was certainly after you. My brother said he was still being followed, and so could not come back to check on you. He has trusted me with your care."

"I don't know how to thank you," Sheila said.

"No problem." Annie waved off Sheila's gratitude.

"What will I do now? I'm afraid that man will kill me, but I am supposed to be on a plane to London."

"Now you must rest. Here you are safe and our night watchman is trustworthy. In the morning, inshallah, we will determine what to do next. My clothing could be helpful if you are trying to hide." She grinned playfully. "It is going to be okay."

"Come with me." Annie led her down the hall to a guest room. Her suitcase already lay on the foot of the bed. Annie pointed out the bathroom then turned to leave. "If you need anything, please do not hesitate to ask."

Sheila was alone. Exhausted, she slipped off her shoes and climbed underneath the covers in spite of the heat. She left the suitcase on her bed and curled up to make space for her feet.

In a few minutes, she was asleep.

Chapter 40
Lochinvar Game Reserve, Zambia
Sunday, March 7

Elephant grass folded down in front as the Landrover crawled over the track. The Lochinvar Game Reserve remained basically unknown and notable mostly for its birds and grasshopper species. Most people don't contract safari companies to see grasshoppers. Besides, rainy season was off-season for tourists.

The grass all but hid the twin tire tracks. Usually, a game warden accompanied visitors to the area, but Aaron Boll had taken a GPS reading on his last trip and they carefully followed the display.

Stuart asked Daniel to drive. Since Sheila had gone, he knew Daniel needed to stay busy and focused if they were to complete their mission. Aaron rode shotgun. They agreed to move into hiding as soon as their weapons arrived, so they could prevent the chance of discovery and get in some much needed practice. As it was, they wasted most of the weekend in Mazabuka watching the news and waiting for word from Chuma to confirm their target.

The order of procession for Friday's parade of dignitaries had been created at the last minute, probably for security reasons. Heads of State would begin arriving Friday morning to attend opening ceremonies at the show grounds. From there, cars would line up in the order determined by Zambia's SADC committee. Chuma had access to the information.

They had three days in Lochinvar and Stuart planned to keep them busy running drills, going over contingency plans, working out angles of approach and egress, and studying maps. It had to be automatic.

"Turn here." Aaron pointed left. After a few minutes, they emerged from the tall grasses onto a plain that sloped down to a river invisible in the marsh reeds. Flocks of wild birds, swirled high into the sky, and settled down again before bursts of color and noise exploded from another sector. Hippos obviously spent nights grazing the plain before returning to the water at daybreak, keeping the grasses cropped. Zambia, like Zimbabwe, still had vast areas largely undiscovered by the outsider; grand tapestries of life, death, and the raw beauty of Africa.

Daniel parked by a lone tree. Aaron climbed to the roof rack and handed down the gear.

Stuart knew mission failure would have major repercussions on their families. He encouraged Daniel to let Sheila go off to London and cool down. Stuart figured she would come around eventually, and he felt safer knowing she was out of harm's way. Hopefully things would work out for them in the end.

Other men would likely have volunteered to be a part of the operation, but Stuart felt more men would needlessly put others in jeopardy without markedly improving their chance of success.

Small. Accurate. Fast. That was the plan, but the next few days would determine the course of history.

Daniel set to raising the tent while Stuart and Aaron scouted for a place to rehearse. Though not especially suited to a perfect field test, Lochinvar would have to suffice. At least they would have no human company.

Stuart knew he would have to trust their ability as marksmen and the quality of their firearms. Both young men grew up hunting in the wilds of Zimbabwe. He already knew they could shoot under stress.

Aaron retrieved a pawpaw from the vehicle. "It's a shame to waste such a good piece of fruit over a bad president." He chuckled and pressed it atop a sharpened stick he hammered into the ground. They marked three spots 1000 yards from the target with stone cairns.

Stuart stood at the final spot and aimed an imaginary gun at their target. With all three shooting the same mark from points on a triangle perimeter, none would be in the cross-fire. They hoped to have the advantage of some elevation, mitigating the possibility of collateral damage.

Daniel secured the lines for the tent fly and Stuart set up a camp table and three chairs. He spread his map, pointed out the lines of fire and pulled out photographs showing where they would sit and wait.

"The parade of dignitaries will be directed through the center of town, past the roundabout at the north end of Cairo Road and then north out of town toward the Hotel." Stuart traced the map with his fingers as he spoke. "According to Chuma, our target will be in vehicle number seven.

"The parade is well publicized and significant crowds are expected along the route to welcome the Heads of State. The procession will move at less than 40 kilometers per hour, giving the big men ample time to smile and wave.

"I will take position at the secondary school, northeast of target. Danny, you'll have the one to the southeast." He pointed to the tidy 'x' on the map due east of target. "And Aaron, you'll be here." His spot on the map sat back almost a block from the parade route. "This is a parking lot. Container trailers usually park along this wall here. From the top of those containers you'll have a clear line between these houses." Stuart traced the alley with his finger all the way to the street.

The men nodded.

"We'll communicate with hands-free headsets. The command string is simple. "Ready. Mark. Fire.""

"How do we know where to aim if his windows are tinted?" Aaron asked.

"Good question. Chuma will call me with his seat position Friday. I'll relay that to you. Mwanyisa typically rides rear right, by the window, but that could change. Our armor piercing rounds should be good from all sides, regardless of where he sits. There is a chance the man will leave his window down, because he likes to hear the accolades. His pride, hopefully, will work against him here."

"How many times do we fire before we split?" Daniel asked.

"I don't know. What do you think?" Stuart had his own opinion, but he knew the more times they fired, the greater the chance of being discovered. He preferred the men decide their own level of risk.

Aaron lit a cigarette and said, "When you hunt an animal, once the shooting begins, everything starts moving faster. Who knows what will happen as soon as the brass starts to fly. There could be secret service men jumping in the way, vehicles accelerating or decelerating."

"So," Daniel said, "regardless of how many shots we take, our first one has to count."

"True," Aaron replied. "But why don't we plan for three. Just a little insurance."

"Danny, what do you think?" Stuart asked.

"Ya. Three is good."

"Okay, then. Here is how we do it. I will call all three like the first. 'Ready. Mark. Fire'. Just like that. If we are right on cue—and we should be for the first—it will be more difficult for them to locate the direction of fire as sound will be coming from all sides. That said, the silencers on these units are quite impressive and with luck, there will be a whole brace of traditional drummers making a bunch of noise for us to get lost in," Stuart said. "The rifles aren't much louder than the bark of a dog."

Stuart pulled out several beers from the cooler. "We can have just this one, but from here on I want straight thinking, okay? No beers after this. There will be plenty of time to celebrate later."

Stuart sat back in his camp chair. A cumulonimbus clawed its way into the sky and the breeze freshened. Stuart took a long pull on his beer. "I've given quite a bit of thought to our exit strategy. The Steyr SSG's have a nice folding stock, so the units can be easily broken down and stowed in a backpack. We'll shoot our three rounds, retrieve the empties, pack our weapons and scram. You guys have both grown up on farms and spent more time on motorbikes than your mothers appreciated, so I know you're comfortable riding. The bikes let you go places cars can't. We'll already have a thousand yard lead, and the crowds will further slow them down, should they spot us and decide to give chase. But remember, a speeding vehicle is usually guilty. Our best chance at getting away is not to be noticed at all. Keep your speed down. Drive the limit, if there is one. Keep to well-concealed roads. These guys may have military air support. If you are the only one driving like a maniac, they'll know you're guilty."

"How are we going to get into position without raising an alarm, or at least without drawing attention to ourselves," Daniel asked. "Three white guys are a bit conspicuous as it is."

"I asked Chuma the same question when we talked this over." Stuart paused as thunder gathered in the distance and rolled growling overhead. "It seems the best way is to arrive in our places just before the target moves into position. Chuma believes the people near our spots will already have moved to spectator areas, leaving the hides under populated. Most people will assume you are there to see the dignitaries. The three of us won't be seen together that day." He nodded at Aaron. "Your dad will truck the bikes to Lusaka this week and deliver them to our pick-up point by Thursday night.

"Study the pictures so you can easily identify your hide and get into place." Stuart handed them pictures of their respective positions. "Any other questions?"

The two younger men stared at the map, visualizing the plan, but saying nothing.

"Good." Stuart raised his beer, "And good luck."

Three bottles clinked in a somber toast as the lightning flashed and rain began to fall.

Chapter 41
Lusaka, Zambia
Early Monday Morning, March 8

Sometime after midnight, Sheila jolted awake. She lay still, listening, trying to remember where she was. Outside the indistinct barking of faraway dogs punctuated the steady gurgle of a garden fountain that sounded like muted wooden chimes.

Yet there was something, some thought had awakened her. It stalked her unconscious. She dared not move for fear she might dislodge it further, making it impossible to recover. She became aware of her legs, cramped because of the suitcase, but she didn't move. Whatever it was jarred her from a deep sleep with so much force she could feel the adrenaline. A bad dream?

No. Something else.

She sat up in bed, working out the cramps and got up to move the suitcase onto the floor.

"Why are you following me?" She spoke to the shadows, remembering the day before. "Why can't you leave me alone?"

A sound outside brought her down against the floor, crouching where she wouldn't be seen. Just the click of a dog's nails as it walked along the concrete gutter that ran along the foundation.

She stayed against the wall, willing herself to remember what it was that so disrupted her sleep. Somewhere in the house she heard a beep, marking the hour.

A familiar dread washed over her as the thought began to materialize in her mind.

"Daniel," she said aloud. "O God. Daniel." The last time she had seen Mpundu, Daniel had been in danger. What now?

In a mad fury of fear she opened the suitcase, groping for her phone. She dialed Daniel's cell, began talking as soon as the call connected.

An automated voice interrupted her. "I'm sorry, the person you are trying to reach has traveled outside of the service area."

She hung up and tried the number for their Mazabuka flat, hoping the line wasn't down.

"Please, please pick up," she whispered into the phone.

Chapter 42
Mazabuka, Zambia
Early Monday Morning, March 8

The ringing next to Daniel's bed startled the crickets and night frogs into silence. Again it rang.

Kathy hurried through the door to the adjoining flat letting the flashlight play across the room until she found the phone.

The ringing stood her flesh on end. She lifted the receiver.

"Daniel?" It was Sheila's voice.

"No luv, it's your mum."

"Mum, where is Daniel? I must speak with—" The line died, words swallowed in an indistinct hiss.

Kathy returned the receiver and flashed her wristwatch. 3:07 a.m. Sheila should be on the plane. Maybe the flight was delayed. Maybe. She stood there, wondering.

Her own flight was scheduled to leave on Wednesday. Stuart had arranged a place in Johannesburg. After Stuart finished his job, they would need to stay out of Zambia for a while. Zimbabwe would be out of the question until investigations closed.

The world seemed to be coming apart too fast. Her daughter, for example, hadn't been herself since this all began. Now their marriage—barely a year old—seemed to be in pieces. But a new marriage isn't supposed to have to deal with assault, and prison, and midnight evacuations. Kathy heard the drums again. Since her meeting with Grace's father, she heard them often. The only problem was that no one else could.

Kathy sighed, turned back toward the door that joined the two flats, and screamed, cutting back the sound with her own hand.

A man stood in the doorway—spear in hand.

"What do you want?" she demanded, her voice steadier than she expected.

The sound of drums and flute and water in her head grew louder. She shone her light into his face. The spear flashed, its razor edge burned the back of her hand. The light dropped and rolled slowly, throwing bizarre moving shadows across white walls.

The man touched the spear to his tongue, tasting her blood.

"U-nodi chii?" She asked again, this time in Shona.

"Daniel Smith."

The noise swirled in her head. Kathy tried to force it back, to concentrate. "He isn't here," she managed.

The sound of feet filled her ears. People running. Drums in sync with her heartbeat, taking over. What is happening to me?

Kathy pressed the cut hand against her chest, blood leaching into her nightgown. She fought her eyes open. Concentrate.

"Va-nodzo-ka rini?" When is he back?

He lowered the spear, the shadow blade follow along the wall until the tip pierced her nightgown and pinched the skin of her stomach.

Drums filled her head. Could he not hear them? "Ha-ndi-ziva. I don't know. Please, you must leave."

A dog barked in the neighbor's yard at the watchman making his rounds. The shadow spear turned and disappeared with the man into the night.

Chapter 43
Lusaka, Zambia
Monday, March 8

Sheila roamed the shady garden and watched color wash the morning sky. She had already missed her flight, and she did not care. Seeing Enoch Mpundu right there in Lusaka completely unnerved her. She thought leaving Zimbabwe would be enough, but it seemed Zimbabwe wouldn't leave them.

The fact that Daniel could be in more danger haunted her, and she couldn't sleep. The brief conversation with her mum, before they were cut off helped some.

She tried to call again on her parent's cell. But all she could do was leave messages and her mum wasn't great about checking. Her dad would check, she knew. She would just have to wait for him.

The dog ambled over and nudged her hand. The roan colored bitch reminded her of Molly—Molly's blood-soaked side and weakly wagging tail. She pushed the thought away. Wanted to kill Mpundu herself.

"Go on. You're not helping. I have to think," she said, trying to sound severe. The dog sat down and scratched, its toenails clipped the tag on its collar, making a rhythmic plinking.

Her host would be up soon. Then she would have to decide what to do. But she didn't want to do anything until she knew Daniel was safe. The fountain gurgled and sputtered from its concrete basin. The gentle sound seemed to block out the world. If only she could stay lost in this corner and believe everything could work out.

She loved Daniel in spite of his determination to go through with his plan. Now, for some reason, she loved him because of it. At first she felt abandoned. Cheated. As if she had woken up and found another woman in his bed. Yet, now she felt cared for by his determination to make things right. Not that she believed it would work. She had to warn him.

She thought of something and pulled out her cellphone. This time she typed a text message to Daniel.

'Enoch in town. Be careful. Call me.' Send.

She hoped it would be delivered when he came within range of a cell tower.

Chapter 44
Kariba Lake, Zambia
Monday Evening, March 8

The hot sun fell in a blaze of orange to be extinguished by the mighty river. A moonless night followed.

The Paradise slipped through inky waters, running without lights toward the dam wall. The wall stretched two thousand feet wide and towered 400 feet over the valley. The submerged gates, each large enough to accommodate four semi-trucks at the same time, were invisible from the lake side of the dam. The Zambezi River Authority regulated the six gates. Though effective in drawing down high waters from seasonal rains, it always resulted in flooding. The spillway gates rarely opened, and then only after authorities evacuated affected flood zones downstream. Usually a quarter of a million people had to move or be moved before the gates opened.

Colette shouldered the air tanks and ran through the pre-dive check, sweltering above water in her wetsuit.

She sat on the bench near the rail, pulled fins over bare feet and snugged the miner's lamp on her forehead. Normally she would check the lamp before hitting water. Not here. Guards patrolled the dam. She placed the air regulator in her mouth, gave Wolfe the all clear and slipped into the lake. Sean Wolfe passed the underwater drill to her with the attached buoyancy control device. The packs would keep the drill from falling straight to the bottom.

Wolfe watched her disappear under water and played out the air line for the pneumatic drill. The drill was awkward on land but manageable in the water. He reached the tape mark on the airline and started the compressor. The compressor needed to run intermittently, and was perhaps the most dangerous part. Noise carried easily across the water and might attract attention.

Wolfe baffled the generator's muffler and the hum sounded like the kapenta boats that crisscrossed the lake every night. These boats headed out from harbor at sunset and hauled in nets of tiny fish that looked like sparkling shards of broken glass. But kapenta boats never fished this close to the dam. Ever.

The compressor satisfied the hungry air tanks and cycled off. Wolfe settled uneasily into the dark silence. It had rained most of the day, with the result that waters flowing from the N'Gatchi-Gatchi river spread a wash of brown silt far out from its point of confluence with the lake, but here the water was clear and Colette would be able to work.

Wolfe shielded a penlight and checked compressor gauges. He had spent the better part of the day pouring over the underwater drill with its circular shaped bits. The shank of the drill extended almost thirty inches. Dual stabilizing handles extended from the body to hold the machine securely in place while the diamond tipped blades bored holes six inches in diameter to a depth of almost three feet.

Colette had quickly grasped the blueprints and seemed confident of finding her marks under water. The compressor switched on. Colette would now be drawing air from the tank, pressing the drill against the concrete face of the dam. Neither of them knew how many times the compressor would cycle on for each hole, but it couldn't be helped. If someone took exception to their proximity to the dam at this time of night, they would probably communicate with machine gun fire. Not a pleasant thought. Perhaps being in the water with the crocodiles was safer.

Wolfe figured security was lax after fifty uneventful years of watching a monstrous concrete structure no one could steal. It was difficult to pay attention to nothing and soldiers found better ways to pass the time.

This didn't provide much consolation; Wolfe would be the first to feel the bullets. The compressor cycled off again. He heard air bubbles. Colette's head broke the black surface, ready for the first plug.

The twelve cardboard cylinders resembled the tube from a roll of paper towels, except they were six inches in diameter and twenty-six inches long. Inside the Dexpan looked not unlike cement mix. Powder dry.

Usually the powder was mixed with water first and then poured into strategically placed holes. The mixture would expand over a period of twelve hours to several times its regular size. The non-explosive demolition agent proved effective on massive concrete and block structures where traditional blasting techniques were inconvenient.

Here the cardboard canisters would saturate after the plugs had been inserted. Because Dexpan required several hours to reach maximum expansion, they would have long enough to move to safety, just in case.

Colette would bore twelve holes in total, one on each of the bottom corners of the six spillway gates to form a horizontal line across the dam's inner face. Finding the holes again in the dark would have been a near impossibility, so Colette inserted a glow-stick in each one after she finished drilling. Following the louvered doors down would bring her close enough to see the cold glow of the green marker peeking from the hole. Then she would remove the light, insert the tube, and start drilling the next hole. It would have been easier to drill all the holes first, but in the event they were discovered before the job was finished, they had agreed to insert the charges as they progressed, though it increased the job time.

They fell into a rhythm: the rush of adrenaline when the compressor kicked on, the bubbles as Colette emerged for another tube. Wolfe watched stars rotate slowly overhead.

Esposito's calculations had been exhaustive. The spillway gates were scheduled to open in a few days. The normal vibrations would accelerate the cracks. When the top of the dam gave way along the line marked by their holes, the excessive rush of water over the top would erode the foundation of the dam on the other side. It would only be a matter of time before water ripped the dam from her footing and sent it plunging forward.

By 2:30am, Colette had already stopped twice to change out her tanks. Each plug weighed better than thirty pounds and she had to leave the drill on the boat or risk dropping the expansive tubes.

Wolfe heard bubbles again and pushed a button on his watch illuminating the dial. She would have to finish quickly in order for them to get away before daybreak. He handed her the last plug and tapped his watch as a time warning. Then she disappeared. He imagined her swimming back to the mammoth wall, removing the glow stick and sliding the tube far into the opening.

A few minutes later she emerged for the last time. He opened the railing gate and dragged her on board.

She spat out her regulator. "Go, go, go. You can get me out of this shit later."

Wolfe started the diesel engines and headed away from the wall.

#

By five a.m. the boat covered enough distance to afford some relief. They both felt exhausted. Their one crewmember—locked in his cabin—had been sleeping thanks to a sedative Colette encouraged him to take for his health the night before.

Wolfe removed the buoyancy compensators from the drill and dumped it with the compressor into the lake. They sank quickly, trailing tiny bubbles in the black water.

Chapter 45
Siavonga, Zambia
Tuesday, March 9

Sean Wolfe and Colette Logan returned to the Eagles Rest after finishing their work on the dam wall. Wolfe said something about 'loose ends' he needed to tie up.

Colette wondered if she were a loose end.

Though she expected her willing participation in the dive had increased his trust in her, she did not like being left in the dark. The sense that Esposito's goal had been loftier than a 'repair job' had grown. Colette wanted proof that he intended the dam to fail badly. She tossed the book she was trying to read and glanced at the clock. It was time to get more information. Wolfe had been gone for twenty minutes, having left just before 5 p.m. Colette rummaged through her bag until she found her lock picks and camera.

Colette pulled on a pair of shorts and left the room. One of the hotel employees stopped sweeping the flagstone walk when he heard her door.

"Good evening, madam," he said. "Shall I get you a drink?" He doubled as bar tender and handyman.

"Thank you, Jared. I would like that. Just cold, bottled water."

"Okay, madam." He smiled, picked up his broom and headed up the walkway behind the chalet.

Wolfe's room sat directly opposite her own. She picked the lock and stepped inside. The curtains were already drawn to keep out the heat.

Near his desk she found a cylinder containing a map, which she spread out on his bed. He did not seem to be overly cautious about hiding evidence. The topographic map had shaded areas illustrating flood zones. Other papers that had been rolled up with the map proved more interesting. One included a copy of an article from The Times of Zambia announcing a scheduled opening of the dam's flood gates. The date and times were highlighted in yellow. Another sheet contained a technical data analysis with a graph indicating the cumulative Richter scale equivalents as each additional gate opened. Not enough.

Colette needed more. Under his pillow, she found a calf-skinned attaché case with a brown envelope inside. Colette moved to the window and peeked out. The waiter had left the water outside her door and started sweeping again just outside their chalets.

"Damn," she whispered. "Go away."

Hurrying back to the envelope, she pulled out the papers and snapped pictures. She moved through the packet as fast as she could, trying desperately to digest its contents.

She had been right. This was much bigger. The Italian planned to destroy the whole dam. Why hadn't Michi told her about this?

Colette returned to the map and traced the Zambezi from the Kariba Dam to the sea, studying the shaded areas again. An eerie horror settled over her mind as she digested the scope of their plan.

It was time to leave.

Chapter 46
Siavonga, Zambia
Tuesday Morning, March 9

Sean Wolfe slid his card across the counter. "I've come to inspect the borehole."

"Just a minute please." The woman left and returned with the same agent who reviewed Wolfe's paperwork before the men did the drilling.

"Good morning, sir," Chalwanda said. "You have come for the borehole?"

"Yes," Wolfe replied. "I have to make my final report."

The man nodded and looked past Wolfe to a group of tourists who had just arrived. Most likely, they wanted a day pass to take the cab across the dam and explore Kariba Heights. The town crowned the hill opposite the gorge. The resorts there still clung to whatever tourist traffic leaked across the border from Zambia.

Wolfe waited for some time before a group showed up that was large enough to distract both of the on-duty agents. He didn't want company. With company came questions.

Wolfe glanced at the tourists clustered around the counter opposite the customs desk, trying to figure out what kind of visa they would need and hopelessly shuffling handfuls of kwacha in an effort to figure out exchange rates.

"Sorry. I see this is a busy time for you," Wolfe said. "If you can show me where they put the hole, I can get out of your way."

Chalwanda glanced at the other guard then nodded. "Come this way." He led Wolfe out a side door and into the hot sun. "It is just there," he said.

"Could you open this gate, so I can bring in my gear?" Wolfe asked.

Chalwanda fished in his pocket for a ring of keys and fiddled with the lock and chain. Wolfe could sense his uncertainty about leaving the gate open to this authorized area. What damage could anyone do? Steal mangos, maybe. Wolfe retrieved a handkerchief from his pocket and made a show of wiping his brow. "It's hot. I'm going to make this quick."

Chalwanda returned to his post.

Wolfe opened the gate and retrieved one long tubular case and a six-inch well cap. He tugged off the temporary cap from the bore and lowered a plumb bob into the hole until it hit bottom.

The red mark on the string hovered just below the bore casing. "Good," he muttered. The hole was a perfect depth to separate the dam foundation from the bedrock. The last Dexpan plug would only cause minor cracks. Should the spillway gates not break as planned, water leaking through these cracks would, over time, cause shifting and eventual dam failure. Esposito admitted it was a long shot. Still, it provided a measure of insurance.

Wolfe opened the case and pulled out the four foot cardboard cylinder and laid it to the side of the borehole. Then he withdrew his string, satisfied that the bottom six feet of the hole contained water. The heavy cylinder slipped into the PVC bore casing the drillers inserted to keep soft earth from collapsing into deeper sections of the well.

Wolfe listened to the whistle of the tube as it traveled the 414 feet to the bottom. When the whistling stopped, Wolfe grabbed the top of the protruding pipe and, with difficulty, pulled out the two foot section of casing. Reaching into the ground, he smeared as much glue as he could on the remaining pipe. Then he applied glue to the cap, reached down the hole and fit this into place effectively sealing off the borehole below ground level.

He kicked dirt down into the hole, removed the flag marking the location of the bore and was done. His shirt soaked with sweat, but he had the same strange feeling of power he felt with his fingers on the switch panel in the control room.

Wolfe packed his tools into the backpack and entered the border office by the side door. The group of tourists he followed in were chatting happily about the little adventure before them. Sean nodded to the agent, who came over.

"I don't know who planned this job, but it is a waste of my time," Wolfe grumbled. "There is no water at all." He fished in his pack for some official looking document, which he presented to Chalwanda for signature. "Sign here, if you would. Just proves I was actually here and didn't write my report while sitting at the bar."

Chalwanda smiled knowingly and signed the paper. Keeping the bosses happy. He returned Wolfe's pen.

They shook hands and Wolfe turned to leave.

"Why did they want to put a borehole here?" Chalwanda called after him. "We already have plenty of water."

173

Wolfe froze, looked past the man, eyes focusing on the president's picture behind the customs counter. He shrugged. "I don't know. Maybe you should ask him."

Chalwanda turned to see the picture of his president and chuckled. When he looked back, the inspector had gone.

Chapter 47
Zambia Flood Zone
Tuesday, March 9

Normally her mother would work the fields, too, but she was late now almost five years. She died in the cold season, Gift remembered. The rains failed that year, and though they had cassava to fill their stomachs, her mother continued to waste away. Gift did not yet understand that disease had eaten the flesh from underneath her mother's skin. She only knew that the drought, which stole her mother's body, had recently entered father, so he could no longer stand.

Before the rains came, he crawled out to the field and, working with a hoe that had been cut in half, continued pressing the maize seed into brown earth until the last staggering rows were planted. That evening he crawled back to his hut and propped himself against the outside wall, resting in the shade with his eyes closed.

For a long time Gift watched, afraid of what might happen next. But she prayed for rain, asked the ancestors to wash away the drought that made her father's arms thin.

When the rains came, she danced in it, let the cold water wash on her face, thrilled the ancestors heard her plea.

Now lorries with soldiers were coming and loading people from the neighboring villages. There was too much rain, they said. "The river will flood. Pack your things."

Too much rain, Gift repeated to herself.

Her grandmother was a mass of wrinkles and stories and superstitions and love. In her gentle old monotone voice she explained everything. How the lorries would come and take them to crowded villages with terrible huts made of fabric so thin it let in the heat. She saw for Gift the long lines of farmers who held out their hands for rations from white and black men in trucks. How the waters would rise quickly, how they would wash away the maize and cassava fields. A farmer without cassava could be pitied, Gift knew. The gods had given them this food because it did not need water to grow and could even be planted in dry season by shoving a cutting into the earth. Without cassava, a village could not survive the lean times.

Grandmother explained with much clucking and head shaking that the river would swallow the graves of Gift's mother and brother and others who had passed. No more would they be able to travel to the burial grounds to speak with them. And even grandmother said it was because there was too much rain.

Gift understood. This was her fault. She had wanted the rain to save her father. She had wanted the rain to chase away the drought in his bones. Now the ancestors had sent so much rain it would take their cassava field and maize field and father would not be strong enough to replant it.

Gift wiped tears from her eyes and went to stand next to her father. Something crowded in her throat.

"Gift. You must pack."

"Father, I have packed," she replied.

"I am grown tired, and I hear the ancestors calling me," he said.

"No, Father. You must not go there. Grandmother said the waters will take the graves of mother and brother and we will not be able to speak to them. If you go there, I will not be able to speak to you either."

"I must talk to that old woman. Stop her foolishness." Father looked up to greet the soldier who approached.

"You must get on the lorry. We are leaving just now." The soldier barked then turned away.

"Gift. I am staying here. The river has always been my friend."

Tears burned her eyes again. "I am sorry, father," she said.

Chapter 48
Siavonga, Zambia
Tuesday, March 9

Massive hydroelectric turbines harnessed power from the Zambezi at the Kariba North power station. It lay hidden, buried mostly underground at the base of the dam. A control room for the spillway gates perched just above it near the foot of the towering white wall. Operation and management of the dam was provided by the Zambezi River Authority, or ZRA. Money for the day-to-day operation was tight. Real profits disappeared long before any filtered down to the control room.

The phone company recently suspended service over unpaid bills, and Beatrice Chiswala, whose job it was to answer the phone, no longer cared. She glanced at the clock.

Quitting time.

Beatrice gathered her belongings, shoved her feet back into stuffy black shoes and waited for her boss to leave. As the station manager, he had done what he could to cut costs. Employees now chipped in to buy their own chicory-flavored coffee. In the good old days sweet buns were delivered every Friday and the refrigerator in the lunchroom kept the Fanta cold.

But sweet buns had not been delivered in quite some time, and the remaining control room employees accepted the changes with silent resignation. At least they were silent until they gathered at the bar for drinks and such entertainment as they could make for themselves.

Beatrice locked the office door after her boss left and smiled to the guard. "Have a good evening, Bodson." They had been romantic until Bodson fell in with some religious group. Now he handed out scary tracts about God's judgment with color pictures of gaunt and emaciated people on their deathbed. Beatrice shuddered.

He still watched her when he thought she wasn't looking, but she preferred less complicated admirers.

Lately, she had noticed a disturbing loss of weight, making her look uncomfortably like the illustrations Bodson's leaflets. At first she did not mind and capitalized on the opportunity to more closely resemble the bodies she saw on the American television programs, but of late, it had grown worse, and she suspected the wasting disease everyone whispered about. She shrugged off the thought and began her walk home.

Her flat was on the dam side of Siavonga town. It was an uncomplicated affair she shared with a young niece who, in exchange for a place to live, served as cook, maid and washerwoman.

In order to keep down the heat, her niece usually did the cooking in the rear yard. Though Beatrice openly made fun of her backward village ways, it was common practice and Beatrice had to admit it was much cooler. Besides, nshima cooked over the fire tasted better.

By now, her niece would have the ground maize and water bubbling in its blackened pot. Yesterday, Beatrice had given the girl money to buy fish at market. Though working in Siavonga office for the ZRA had few benefits, fish was plentiful, and Beatrice was hungry.

The winding, dirt footpath roughly mirrored the shoreline before turning uphill toward her flat.

Beatrice heard the sound of someone walking among a grove of banana trees as she passed. When she turned to look, something smashed into the back of her head. Her vision went black before her body hit the ground.

#

Sean Wolfe dragged the woman into the grove of trees. He pulled the keys from her handbag and covered the body with dead banana fronds. It was the first time he had hit a woman with a club, and he found the experience tactile and satisfying. He was surprised when the woman started to snore, and he turned her head to open the airways and keep her quiet.

After nightfall Wolfe left the grove, making a mental note to next time find a hiding place with fewer spiders. Wolfe followed the path downhill, toward the building that served as the dam control room. A buzzing security light masked the sound of his approach.

The night-guard moved his metal folding chair to the far edge of the lighted area to avoid the swarm around the floodlight. He leaned over his Bible, stopping occasionally to brush bugs from the pages.

Wolfe stepped into the perimeter of light and strode quickly to the guard, smiling broadly as if they were old friends.

"Good evening." Wolfe reached as if to give a friendly pat on the man's shoulder, his hand concealing a syringe with five-milligrams

180

of Estazolam. The needle penetrated the guard's clothing and delivered the dose before the sting registered.

"You must leave the premises." The guard reached up to scratch his arm.

"Don't you just hate those damn mosquitoes?" Wolfe said, ignoring the direction. "I'm surprised your boss doesn't give you a net." He shook his head, turned to face the swirl of bugs around the light. "Terrible."

The guard tried again. "I'm ordering you to leave. This property is government." A puzzled look crossed the guard's face, aware of a numbing sensation between his ears.

"Yes. I'll be leaving in a minute." Wolfe reached into the backpack at his side and held up a beer. "Would you like a drink?"

Bodson stared, fighting to recognize it. The Bible slipped, sprawled out on the dirt. He fell hard to his chair.

Wolfe opened the bottle and tucked it between the guard's knees as he slumped over and tumbled to the ground. Sean opened another and lay it near the man's upturned hand where the liquid gurgled and foamed into the dirt.

Wolfe surveyed his work. "Sorry to hear about your drinking problem."

He pulled the woman's keys and opened the door.

The rest should be easy. Wolfe walked past the secretary's desk to the control room. Identical levers situated in a row were labeled 'One' through 'Six.' They controlled hydraulic louvers that shuttered the spillway gates. Wolfe unscrewed a yellow switchboard cover and lifted it off.

According to Esposito, only three of the gates were ever opened at one time. The release of that much water caused excessive vibrations and dam engineers had observed a dangerous oscillating wave pattern develop with all six gates open. They quickly limited the use to three.

Because of unseasonably high rainfalls, the River Authority planned to open the three gates Thursday of that week. Evacuation efforts were already underway. Of course, it was pointless. The actual flood when the dam broke would be cataclysmic.

Wolfe smiled. Exploiting a weakness. So simple it was a wonder no one tried it before. He silently congratulated the Italian.

Behind the yellow panel, a series of black wires led to and from the gate controls. Wolfe clipped the wires for the three unused levers—spill gates four, five and six. He pulled black wire and timing devices from his pack and installed a bypass. When he was done, the levers for gates one, two and three would each open another as well. Timers ensured the unused gates only opened thirty seconds after the first three. Time for spray to fill the basin, blocking the controller's view.

With all six gates opened the dam would vibrate under the pressured release of almost 570 thousand cubic meters of water per minute, setting the dam on a course of self-destruction.

The danger of a full-open situation was not widely known. None of the usual spectators atop the dam would notice a problem. The controller himself wouldn't be able to see. Spray from even one gate engulfed the entire spillway basin much like the over-spray of Victoria Falls.

Wolfe walked to the observation window and allowed himself a moment to imagine the proceedings.

In his mind, he could see the explosion of white from the gates above him, feel the way the earth would tremble with the force of water pressing through the opening. The expansive demolition mix had already completed its work. Though not sufficient in itself to destroy the dam, the new cracks weakened the dam and set the perfect table for a disaster.

Wolfe ran his hands over the switches, aware that a flick of his fingers would erase millions of lives. This was bigger than the Christmas tsunami in 2004. The feeling of power was intoxicating.

It would be the greatest flood since the days of Noah.

Wolfe closed his backpack, locked up the control room and walked past the sleeping guard. He retraced his steps until he found the woman moaning softly in the grove of spongy trees.

"It is hard to find reliable employees these days." He threw the keys into the leaves next to her.

Chapter 49
Zanzibar, Tanzania
Wednesday, March 10

Colette arrived in Zanzibar by ferry. Several young men on board eyed her with interest, but she didn't care. She was on vacation. Michi contacted her about another job. Told her to wait. Assured her it wouldn't be long.

Zanzibar rested off the mainland of Tanzania, a paradise frequented by European tourists. Those who came, booked holidays here because of the exotic east African flare.

A perfect hiding place.

She walked out of her room and sat down on a rattan chair under the pavilion. Her room, built on pilings at the end of a pier, had been booked by one of Michi's contacts and boasted a magnificent view of the bay. A local dhow, leaning on its pontoon, plied the waters under a triangular sail.

The palm walls of her room creak slightly in the sea breeze. A comforting sound. Colette sipped a rum and coke and wondered what Michi had in mind for her next. She expected it might involve clean up after the Kariba job. Her take on the job had been well in excess of one million US dollars. Maybe she would retire.

Time would tell.

She had been angry that Sean Wolfe had kept the truth from her about what they were doing in Kariba. Would it have made any difference?

Maybe Michi was trying to protect her.

Protect her from what? Himself?

After the next job, she would disappear for a while. Maybe a long while. She was ready for a real vacation. A vacation where she could go home and sleep in her own bed.

Chapter 50
Lochinvar Game Reserve, Zambia
Wednesday, March 10

Three exhausted men sank onto their sleeping mats in the tent.

Since Monday, they had each burned through almost 500 rounds of ammunition. Stuart Hall drilled them incessantly, made them break down their rifles, rehearse escape plans, recite alternate routes. After sunset, Stuart ran situation drills, planning for every conceivable contingency. They knew the plan forward and backward.

He had taken the raw talent of two young men and molded them into a team. They arrived knowing how to hunt and shoot. They would leave as a functioning tactical unit.

The men listened to hippos calling along the river bank, aware that the next few days would determine the destiny of a nation, and their own.

"Men," Stuart said, "you are ready. Remember, this is Africa; do not expect anything to go according to plan."

Chapter 51
Kariba Dam
Thursday, March 11

Cars arrived early. Crowds positioned themselves where they might best see the flood gates open. The top of the dam opened for the parade of cameras, sun tan lotion and coolers. Fat dripping from thick coils of boerewors sausage sizzled on portable grills. Local vendors hustled, hawking everything from dried kapenta and roasted peanuts to matching sets of ebony-carved elephants polished with floor wax.

Local women selling crocheted table cloths and doilies bantered good-naturedly with each other; their wares draped over branches to form stands that braced themselves against the press of tourists and sightseers and curio shoppers. Prices varied according to skin color and bartering was expected. Six-foot tall giraffes, carved from a single piece of local wood stared down at the craftsman who busied himself carving another.

The festive mood carried from those parked along the banks above the dam to those across the wall itself. They toasted the event with pink plastic jugs of fruit-flavored maheu and brown glass bottles of Zambia's Mosi beer.

Today the Kariba Dam would become a spectacular cascade, finding its place temporarily among the greatest falls in the world.

#

Downstream, the opening of the spillway gates precipitated the evacuation of 250,000 people and meant the loss of hundreds of acres of farmland. Though the Zambezi River Authority had arrangements with the World Health Organization and UNICEF to distribute relief aid to people temporarily displaced, the flooding destroyed houses and erased ox trails, footpaths and roads. The flood stole the memory of a place, and free handouts from the WHO or UNICEF did nothing to compensate a villager and his children for the loss of favorite haunts and important landmarks.

Just above the flood zone, temporary camps had been established so people could be returned to their decimated lands as quickly as possible. The media arrived to promote the efficiency and compassion of the World Health Organization and UNICEF. Production deadlines would be met, and headlines would be written and emailed to editors who would weigh the stories for space against international news. The world had almost become immune to the parade of sad black faces passing briefly across their television screens before broadcasters read the daily check on sports. Other snips and sound bites of the NGO's solid compassion would make its way into the propaganda of their mission.

Evacuating the banks of the Zambezi to accommodate the opening of three spillway gates involved a relatively small area. But water meant life, and all over Africa people were drawn to it. Zones likely to flood only when the great concrete dam opened its mouth every 20 or 30 years were quickly repopulated and village life started over.

For weeks since the ZRA made the announcement, military and humanitarian groups worked furiously to load entire villages into waiting trucks to move them just above the projected high water mark. Calabashes of beer were lifted carefully into lorries where wide-eyed children held them between knees. Watery-eyed, old men with axes hanging from their shoulders climbed in after, scolding the children to be careful with the beer.

Before the lorries came, people scrambled to bag the year's increase of maize, sweet potatoes and bleached cassava root. Burlap bags bulged with raw, unshelled peanuts and household goods bristled in bundles. Tins of kerosene leaked beside picketed goats and assorted plastic containers holding wild honey. Chickens—hobbled to each other—lay sprawled and blinking on the hot earth by enamelware basins and bundles tied in local cloth full of the stuff of everyday village life.

Huge camps catered to the press of temporary refugees as trucks continued to arrive, adding more bewildered people to the melee.

A few village elders remembered a time before the dam. Floods had been predictable then. They could watch the sky and the creatures and know it was time to move to higher ground. They did not have to listen to a radio, or wait for green military lorries to bring them word.

The people who now controlled the river must have some powerful magic, indeed. Still, the elders wondered how long men, even powerful men, could stand against the might of Nyaminyami. Soon the river god would grow angry, throw off its harness and be mastered by no one. So the old men talked and smoked crude pipes and remembered.

And still more trucks arrived.

Somewhere it had rained too much. Somewhere there were people now who could say with certainty when, and how much water would come. They could put pink plastic ribbons on trees and say, 'the water will not rise beyond this tree.' And the people moved, knowing the water would not pass the pink talismans.

What medicine man could compete with this kind of magic?

Chapter 52
Kariba Dam
Thursday, March 11
3:54 p.m.

Many of the Zambezi's riverine tribal groups celebrate a coming-up-from-the-water ceremony. Perhaps the most famous is the Kuomboka. People from all across the Western Province gather annually to see the pomp and circumstance of the Lozi King moving his home as flood-waters rise. Anderson Kalyangu sighed. He would miss the ceremony this year. Miss the bold black and white striped royal barge; the entourage—paddling furiously lest they be thrown overboard; the matching white t-shirts; the local drums. The price of traveling to the other side of Zambia had been prohibitive. If the roads between Siavonga and Mongu—the capital of Zambia's Western Province—would be repaired, then Anderson Kalyangu might have been able to go.

Instead he had to work. But this wasn't so bad. Today he was as important as the Lozi King.

At ten that morning, Kalyangu had received a call on his cellphone from the Zambezi River Authority's main office in Lusaka. It was his boss.

"Good morning, Kalyangu. We have final clearance for a release today at sixteen hundred hours. The evacuations are complete. Remember, we have permission to release for only 30 minutes. More than that and the river will rise above the prescribed height."

Kalyangu had been told all of this before.

"Your assistant is with you?" his boss asked.

"Yes, sir." Kalyangu lied. Beatrice sent word the day before explaining that she had been hurt and would not be in to work for the rest of the week. She frequently made excuses of late, but Kalyangu didn't mind if she took the day without pay. He would enter her in the log book anyway, and collect her wage. Not a bad deal. After all, he had to do her work as well.

"Is everything ready?"

"Everything is ready," Kalyangu replied.

He stared out the control room window. Not a bad trade for missing the Kuomboka this year. He swallowed hard, studied the top of the wall, absently trying to count the people crowded along the edge.

Four minutes to release.

It would have been better if he had not been troubled by night terrors. Water roared, the earth vibrated and mist shrouded his room. Every time the roar and spray and trembling increased until he grabbed the iron frame of his low bed to steady himself. Each time the terror came, he thought he had died.

But Kalyangu would awaken to the gentle squeak of fruit bats or the drip of rain from the eves. He would wipe water or sweat—he was never sure—from his face and lay for a long time in the darkness until the adrenaline wore off. Not once had he been able to convince himself it was only a dream.

Kalyangu shook off the feeling and glanced at the clock. He arranged himself in the controller's chair feeling a rush of pride.

One minute to open.

He placed his fingers on levers for spillway gates One, Two and Three. The clock on the wall ticked away the last few seconds. Levers for gates Four, Five and Six had long ago been covered with black electrical tape: a warning to never use them. In his mind, the rumbling of his night terrors started again. The clocked marked off the last seconds to open. He would make a spectacle to compete with the Victoria Falls.

Three. Two. One.

Anderson Kalyangu slid the three levers slowly to a full-open position. Sleeping hydraulics came to life, turned massive louvers. The wall erupted in a rage of white as geysers exploded from flood gates simultaneously opening several hundred feet over the spillway basin.

Thirty seconds later, the last three gates opened behind a screen of spray with the whine of more hydraulics that no one could hear.

The river god snarled through the restraint. People cheered. Spray filled the air, covering skin and hair with droplets like dew on grass. Several million tons of concrete shook from the mighty rush of water through it. A few people shared questioning glances.

Surely it had to be safe. After all, the dam had been built by the British, right?

Over 150 kilometers away, a seismograph shot chaotic lines across a white paper roll. After three minutes, the erratic rhythm coalesced into a single synchronized wave. Regional seismographs automatically transmitted the data via radio frequency to the ZRA monitoring office in Lusaka.

Almost immediately, the shaking forced a subterraneous crack between the dam and its bedrock anchor. Water pressed in. Slow, persistent, determined.

Soon other filament cracks formed on the reservoir side at the bottom corner of spillway gate four. Invisible to spectators, these cracks spread horizontally toward adjacent flood gates, continuing across the dam face.

Anderson Kalyangu sat back on the bar stool and watched nervously as minutes ticked by. He had tried a pair of binoculars, but the overspray covered his observation window. The roar of falling water engulfed the room.

Thirty minutes was a long time.

Kalyangu tried to distract himself, to calculate the volume in his head but got lost in the zeros. He had always been good at math. He walked to a nearby desk to get a ballpoint pen and a notepad. The vibrations under his feet felt eerily like the night terrors.

Back in his chair, he wrote numbers on the pad, added three commas. He couldn't concentrate and scribbled it out. It wasn't his job anyway. He put the pad and pen on top of the control panel. Within seconds, tremors sent the pen to the floor. He stooped to pick it up and the notepad followed, hitting him on the head.

Something isn't right, he thought. He pressed his face close to the glass, trying to see the dam. Nothing but spray. The trembling gained strength.

Anderson Kalyangu reached for his cell. It showed a missed call from the corporate office. Funny. He hadn't heard it ring. He punched the green button and pressed a finger into his open ear, trying to find a place where he might be able to hear. He stepped into the bathroom and shut the door. The toilet lid clattered against the enamel basin; water splattered in the bowl. The cell screen showed that the call had gone through. Again he pressed the phone to his head, trying to hear something, anything.

"Hello," he said, almost yelling. "There is too much vibration. What should I do?"

A voice answered—someone speaking indistinctly far away, but that was all.

This morning he had been looking forward to the event. Now he couldn't wait for it to be over. Ten minutes in. Twenty minutes to go. I am just being a frightened school girl, he thought.

He stepped from the lavatory, walked to the window. Water on glass ran in rivulets as if it were raining. Perhaps it *was* raining. He tried to remember if there had been clouds.

Trembling fingers typed out a text message to his boss's cellphone. The ZRA office phone couldn't receive text. He hoped his boss had his phone nearby.

'*Too much shaking. Please advise to close gates*'. He clicked the send button and waited.

Fourteen minutes left. Kalyangu stared at the phone's black screen.

He paced the office. Picked up the office phone. No service, he remembered. Not that it mattered. He couldn't hear anyway.

After a few minutes, he returned to the control room. A mug crashed to the floor throwing cold coffee and shattered glass. The shards quivered like landed fish across the vibrating concrete.

It was too much.

He glanced at the clock: 16:21. Twenty one minutes open.

Anderson Kalyangu grabbed his phone.

A message. Two words.

'Stop Gate'.

Kalyangu scrambled for the panel, threw all switches to 'closed'. The hydraulic louvers turned against water in the spillway gates. Within a few seconds the vibrations disappeared.

Anderson slumped into a chair and wiped beaded sweat from his face.

Chapter 53
Bombay, India
Thursday, March 11

The train lumbered along the eastern edge of the Indian sub-continent, stopping here and there to disgorge passengers and take on new chattering masses. Sean Wolfe closed his eyes and felt the wind. He'd purchased a pair of Kurta Pajama's in Mumbai. With a newly shaved head and his mother's Mediterranean blood, he blended reasonably well into the surroundings. His Kurta was cleaner than most of those who sat atop the train on the way south to Ratnagiri, but he didn't care. It would do for now.

It was a pity, he mused, that he had not had more time with Colette Logan. He wondered where she had gone. He was disappointed, though not surprised, when he returned to the Eagles Rest and found her missing. She was something of an enigma. A capable operative wrapped up in stunning, natural beauty. Perhaps with more time… He let the thought die in his mind. It would never do to keep a list of regrets. Especially in his line of work.

Wolfe was glad to be back in India. The incredible press of humanity made it easier to hide, and few people bothered about him.

Thankfully, he could get by in most places with English and his faltering Hindi, which was, he admitted, quite terrible.

The train slowed. Mango trees grew in thick clusters by fields of another seaside community. Ratnagiri figured as close to home as any place. His cottage, a simple affair with breezy windows and a well-screened porch, held his few worldly belongings.

He would swim, fish, read and visit with a few local women until someone posted a message for him online. Then he would pack up and head off to work again.

Chapter 54
Lusaka, Zambia
Thursday, March 11
5:00 a.m.

The night watchman rolled his last cigarette. Trevor Chilano allowed himself one, every two hours. It helped pass the time. He lit a match. Every hour he would walk the perimeter of the property before returning to his stool in the corner of the front yard. His employer, a Muslim businessman, provided a fair income and had been thoughtful enough to construct a shelter against rain. From this position in the back corner of the garden, Chilano could see all the way to the far wall on both sides. On his right the fountain, and on his left a vegetable garden. It wasn't a bad job. The boredom was the worst, but his employer paid him a bonus every month, and the work was steady.

Chilano pulled the smoke deep into his lungs and tried to relax. The dog lay sleeping against the house. The day guard wouldn't arrive until 7 am, if he were on time. Chilano tried not to think about the man who had visited him after work. The man seemed quite interested in his job and wanted to know if his employer had any open positions. The press of questions included the number of people he had to watch and who lived there. It had all seemed fine, until the man pressed a US twenty dollar bill into his hand and asked about the white woman.

It was probably nothing.

The gate shack also had a tin roof, but this place had more air, and Chilano preferred it. For the first time in a week, there had been a night without rain in Lusaka. He didn't mind the rain. Sometimes he slept, leaning against the back wall on his stool, listening to the sound of rain on tin. Nobody went out in the rain after dark. Even thieves don't like getting wet.

His cigarette burned down to his fingers before he ground it out under his heel. He stood. Stretched. Ready to begin his rounds. The dog ignored him.

He hissed for the animal. "Come."

Still the dog slept.

He spat into the grass and moved off, jealous of the dog. A shadow moved in his mind, but he ignored it. He stopped at the fountain, cupped water to his mouth with his hands. Two hours to go. He splashed his face awake.

At the front corner of the property, he turned.

Where is that dog? He thought. Sometimes it would ignore him when he started his rounds, but never for long. Chilano had grown accustomed to the mongrel bitch skipping along beside him with only one ear at attention.

He wanted another cigarette already. Sigh.

Chilano completed the circle by himself and sat down in his shack. All in order. Two hours until quitting time. The thing moved again in his mind. He looked toward the dog and whistled softly. It didn't move.

If the dog was sleeping, he could, too.

At six o'clock, two men climbed over the wall. One of the men sang to himself, notes rising and falling around the bubbling fountain. The leader motioned the singer off toward the dozing guard, and he turned to the house. He searched around the stone planter filled with thorny bougainvillea until he found the key. The day guard had been more talkative after a few beers.

A dull thump came from the watchman's corner. It sounded like an overripe pawpaw melon falling to the ground.

Enoch Mpundu entered the house and headed toward the master suite. A couple lay under a thin tangled sheet, while an oscillating fan played back and forth across their sleeping bodies. Pity he did not have more time, he thought. He pulled a .45 automatic colt pistol from his belt, pressed the steel to the man's forehead, and waited for his eyes to open.

"Where is the woman?" Enoch whispered.

The fog of sleep cleared; the man stared at the intruder but said nothing.

"Perhaps you did not hear me." Enoch moved the barrel, pressing it hard against the man's nose.

"I do not know what you are talking about." The man whispered, but his voice carried little conviction. The woman stirred.

"I am sorry to hear that." Enoch pulled the trigger.

Gunfire shattered the room's silence. Its effect on the sleeping woman was electric. She convulsed out of sleep, eyes wide, as if she herself had been shot. Impossibly, her husband moaned, his back arching then relaxed. Blood soaked into the pillow behind his head.

The woman's chest heaved in panic. Enoch swung the barrel toward the woman and repeated his question.

"Where is the white woman?"

Annie grasped the sheet, pulled it around her. She touched her husband, feeling his warmth, knowing it would not last long. Rage crept in and blurred her vision. She faced her husband. Spoke to him. "This man has taken your life, but in exchange he will receive the judgment of God." Shock took hold and Annie turned back to the man with the gun and began to laugh.

"You are a fool." Mpundu drew back the weapon and hit her across the face. Then she fell silent.

He moved down the hall, checking on either side as he went. A lock blocked his way to the last room. He pounded on the door. Heard nothing. Backing up, he raised his booted foot and kicked the door, breaking it open.

Chapter 55
Lusaka, Zambia
Thursday, March 11
6:04 a.m.

Sheila was already awake when she heard the gunshot. In the last few days, she had done nothing but stay within the gardened walls, waiting to hear back from Daniel. Wanting to know he was safe. She wondered if the paranoia would ever go away. But the gunshot was real enough, and she knew what it meant. Mpundu had come for her—the demon escaping again from her nightmares.

Without taking time to dress, she stood on the bureau by her bed and climbed onto the windowsill. The security bars on the window precluded any escape by that way but provided a good handle. From the windowsill she crawled to the top of a wardrobe opposite her bed and pushed against the attic access panel. What rats and spiders she might find up there mattered little now. The panel stuck for a moment, and a familiar panic clouded her mind. Perhaps she should just leave by the door and run for her life. But a man with the gun was out there and even if she managed to make it out of the house, the gate would be locked, and he would get to her before she could find the key.

Crouching on the wardrobe on all fours, she put her back up against the panel and pushed with her legs and arms. Black attic dirt showered around her and the panel gave way. Lifting it off to the side, she clambered in, praying the dirt wouldn't give her away. A man pounded on the door of her room. She knelt on the rafters, tried to slide the panel back into place. It stuck on something. Fear clawed at her resolve. She fought the urge to leave the panel, to flee deeper into the attic. But the open ceiling would surely be noticed. There was no other way out. She ran her hands around the edge of the panel and found where it was jammed under a ceiling joist. She wiggled it back and forth, ignoring wood biting into her knees.

The panel loosened, slid back into its place with a gentle thump. She heard the bedroom door crash open. Sheila clung awkwardly to the rafters, holding her breath.

"Woman." The voice of her night terror carried up to her. "When we first met, you were very forward. Now you are playing hard to get?"

A short chuckle followed and the sound of him digging through her suitcase. A familiar darkness pressed closer. She had re-entered her nightmare. Sheila bit into her forearm, tasting her own salty blood.

Chapter 56
South of Lusaka, Zambia
Thursday, March 11

Daniel Smith steered the Landrover off the bush track and onto the tar road, finishing the first jolting leg of their journey out of Lochinvar.

Aaron Boll settled low in the back seat determined to get some rest before they reached town and split up in preparation for their mission. They said little, preoccupied with the next twenty-four hours.

Daniel slowed to select shallower potholes in a particularly pitted section of road. Images of Sheila crowded his mind. He wasn't sure where things would go from here. For a while, he would need to lay low. If their operation succeeded, the entire power structure of Zimbabwe would dissolve, with perhaps a few ill-conceived attempts by the more powerful cabinet ministers to grab some kind of control.

But that was not his problem.

The population feared Mwanyisa, but few loved him. Any inquisition for the assassins would go away quickly. Most would wonder why no one had done it before. Then, perhaps, Daniel thought, he would be free to find Sheila and salvage something from their failing marriage. If it wasn't already too late.

Sheila had only been a girl when her daddy went off to war with the Selous Scouts, fighting communist backed rebels in the country. Something in that left its mark on her. It was a tender place he had wounded again when he volunteered to help make this little, private war. Stuart had probably been right. As soon as Mwanyisa found out where they had gone, they weren't really safe, even in Zambia. If Mwanyisa's government had been willing to use them as leverage to get what they wanted, they would do it again. More than that, if things went wrong tomorrow, Sheila would have been in considerable danger if she stayed in Zambia. So he let her go, let her run off to England. Now, what he wanted more than anything, was to go after her.

Damn, he thought. What a mess.

They passed a communications tower and several satellite dishes incongruously surrounded by huts and groves of banana trees. They weren't far from Lusaka now. Beside him Stuart pulled his phone and turned it on. He typed in his password and held the display screen back to compensate for his eyes. One voice message from Davison Chuma.

He patted Daniel on the shoulder. "Better pull over, so I can hear this."

Daniel stopped the Landrover. Stuart dialed in and listened to the sound of Chuma's voice.

A man on his bicycle approached the vehicle curiously. His face appeared briefly at the window, then passed. Stuart closed the phone and stared straight ahead.

"Dad?" Something was wrong.

The phone lay closed on Stuart's lap. "Kathy's been attacked. They were looking for you, Danny." He spoke in monotone.

Aaron immediately came to attention. "What the hell –?"

"She's safe, thank God. Chuma isn't sure, but thinks it was Mpundu, or one of his squad." Stuart's face lost its color.

"I thought mum was in Johannesburg," Daniel said.

"She is now. It happened in Mazabuka before she left." He turned to Daniel. "Better check your phone."

Stuart opened his door, stepped out to call Chuma. The man's great shoulders sagged.

Daniel cursed himself and his phone as it powered up too slowly, his mind imagining the worst. Wishing he had taken her to Lusaka himself. Seen her off. With an effort he controlled his fingers to retrieve the two text messages from Sheila waiting in his inbox. Aaron, leaned forward from the back seat, reading over his shoulder.

The first was from Monday, four days ago. *'Enoch in town. Be careful. Call me.'*

"What the hell is going on? She was supposed to be in England by Monday," Daniel said.

He selected the next message, sent that day. His hands turned clammy. The message was signed 'E. Mpundu.' Daniel read it again. Trying to take it in.

Would you like to make a trade? You for your woman.

Daniel closed the phone, pressed his forehead against the steering wheel and ran his fingers into his hair. "Oh God. What now?"

Stuart appeared in the doorway. "How is Sheila?"

"Mpundu has her," Daniel's voice shook, barely controlled.

207

Stuart gripped the seat. Fought words from his mouth. "Is she okay?"

"I don't know," Daniel said.

"What does he want?"

Daniel looked at his father-in-law and shrugged. "Me."

Books by this author include:

The Zambezi Chronicles
      The Contract *
      Critical Fault *
      Cover of Darkness

and

The Moderator Series
      The Moderator
      The Coma
      Grid Lock

*Now available in audio from Audible.com or iTunes.com.

\#

ww.facebook.com/dwightkoppbooks.com

Acknowledgments

I am thankful for the editing assistance of Doe Kopp, Colin Wilcox, Michael Long, Martha Squaresky and Jay Squaresky. My book is better because of their input.

Any remaining errors are, of course, entirely my fault.

www.ingramcontent.com/pod-product-compliance
Lightning Source LLC
Chambersburg PA
CBHW070825120626
46556CB00002B/654